THE YOUNG
LION HUNTER

THE YOUNG LION HUNTER

ZANE GREY

G.K. Hall & Co. • Chivers Press
Thorndike, Maine USA   Bath, England

This Large Print edition is published by G.K. Hall & Co., USA
and by Chivers Press, England.

Published in 1998 in the U.S. by arrangement with
Golden West Literary Agency.

Published in 1998 in the U.K. by arrangement with
Golden West Literary Agency.

U.S. Softcover   0-7838-0345-1   (Paperback Series Edition)
U.K. Hardcover   0-7540-3507-7   (Chivers Large Print)
U.K. Softcover   0-7540-3508-5   (Camden Large Print)

The text of this Large Print edition is unabridged.
Other aspects of the book may vary from the original edition.

Set in 16 pt. Plantin by Rick Gundberg.

Printed in the United States on permanent paper.

British Library Cataloguing in Publication Data available

Library of Congress Cataloging in Publication Data

Grey, Zane, 1872–1939.
    The young lion hunter / Zane Grey.
      p. cm.
    ISBN 0-7838-0345-1 (lg. print : sc : alk. paper)
    1. Large type books. I. Title.
  PS3513.R6545Y69 1998
    813′.52—dc21   98-34455

CONTENTS

THE
YOUNG LION HUNTER

CHAPTER I

KEN WARD'S ARRIVAL IN UTAH

"Dick, I shore will be glad to see Ken," said Jim Williams, in his lazy drawl. "I reckon you'll be, too?"

Jim's cool and careless way of saying things sometimes irritated me. Glad to see Ken Ward! I was crazy to see the lad.

"Jim, what you know about being glad to see any one isn't a whole lot," I replied. "You've been a Texan ranger all your life. I've only been out here in this wild, forsaken country for three years. Ken Ward is from my home in Pennsylvania. He probably saw my mother the day he left to come West. . . . Glad to see him? Say!"

"Wal, you needn't git peevish. Now, if we calkilated right from Ken's letter he'll be on to-day's stage — an' there she comes bowlin' round the corner of the Pink Cliffs."

I glanced up eagerly, my eye sweeping out on the desert, climbing the red ridge to see a cloud of dust rolling along the base of the great walls.

"By Jingo! You're right, Jim. Here she comes. Say, I hope Ken is aboard."

Jim and I were sitting on a box in front of a store in the little town of Kanab, Utah. The day before we had ridden in off Buckskin Mountain, having had Ken Ward's letter brought out to us by one of the forest rangers. We had a room in a cottage where we kept what traps and belongings we did not need out on the preserve; and here I had stored Ken's saddle, rifle, lasso, blanket — all the things he had used during his memorable sojourn with us on Penetier the year before. Also we had that morning sent out to one of the ranches for Ken's mustang, which was now in a near-by corral. We intended to surprise Ken, for it was not likely we would forget how much he cared for that mustang. So we waited, watching the cloud of dust roll down the ridge till we could see under it the old gray stage swaying from side to side.

"Shore, he mightn't be aboard," said Jim.

I reproached myself then for having scorned Jim's matter-of-fact way. After all there was no telling from Jim's looks or words just how he felt. No doubt he looked forward to Ken's visit as pleasurably as I. We were two lonely forest rangers, seldom coming to the village, and always detailed to duty in the far solitudes of Coconina Preserve, so that the advent of a lively and companionable youngster would be in the nature of a treat.

The stage bumped down over the last rocky steps of the ridge, and headed into the main street of Kanab. The four dusty horses trotted along with a briskness that showed they knew they had reached the end of their journey.

"There's a red-headed kid sittin' with the driver," remarked Jim. "Leslie, thet can't be Ken."

"No, Ken's hair is light. . . . There he is, Jim. . . . There's Ken. He's looking out of the window!"

The horses clattered up and stopped short with a rattle and clink of trappings, and a lumbering groan from the old stage. Somebody let out a ringing yell. I saw the driver throw off a mail-pouch. Then a powerful young fellow leaped over the wheel and bounded at me. "Dick Leslie!" he yelled. I thought I knew that yellow hair, flying up, and the keen eyes like flashes of blue fire. But before I could be sure of anything he was upon me, had me in a bear hug that stopped my breath. Then I knew it was Ken Ward.

"Oh, Dick, maybe I'm not glad to see you!" Whereupon he released me, which made it possible for me to greet him. He interrupted me with eager pleasure, handing me a small bundle and some letters. "From home, Dick — your mother and sister. Both well when I left and tickled to death that I was going to visit you. . . . Why — hello, Jim Williams!"

"Ken, I shore am glad to see you," replied Jim, as he wrung and pumped Ken's hand. "But I wouldn't 'a' knowed you. Why, how you've growed! An' you wasn't no striplin' when you trimmed the Greaser last summer. Ken, you could lick him now in about a minnit."

"Well, maybe not quite so quick," replied Ken, laughing. "Jim, I've taken on fifteen or twenty pounds since I had that scrap with the Greaser, and I've had a season's training under the most famous football and baseball trainers in the world."

"Wal, now, Ken, you're shore goin' to tell me all about thet," said Jim, greatly interested.

To me Ken Ward had changed, and I studied him with curious interest. The added year sat well upon him, for there was now no suggestion of callowness. The old frank, boyish look was the same, yet somewhat different. Ken had worked, studied, suffered. But as to his build, it was easy to see the change. That promise of magnificent strength and agility, which I had seen in him since he was a mere boy, had reached its fulfilment. Lithe and straight as an Indian, almost tall, wide across the shoulders, small-waisted and small-hipped, and with muscles rippling at his every move, he certainly was the most splendid specimen of young manhood I had ever seen.

"Hey, Kid, why don't you come down?" called Ken to the boy on top of the stage. "Here's Dick Leslie — you remember him."

I looked from the boy to Ken.

"It's my brother Hal," responded Ken. "Father wanted me to bring him along, and Hal has been clean mad ever since I was out West last

10

year. So, Dick, I had to bring him. I expect you'll be angry with me, but I couldn't have come without him. I wanted him along, too, Dick, and if it's all right with you —"

"Sure, Ken, it's all right," I interrupted. "Only he's pretty much of a kid — has he got any sand?"

"He's all sand," replied Ken, in a lower voice. "That's the trouble; he's got too much sand."

Ken called to his brother again and the youngster reluctantly clambered down. Evidently the meeting with Ken's ranger friends was to be an ordeal for Hal. I seemed to remember his freckled face and red head, but not very well. Then he dropped over the wheel of the stage, and came toward me readily, holding out his hand.

"Hullo, Dick, I remember you all right," he said.

I replied to his greeting and gave the lad a close scrutiny. I should say fourteen years would have topped his age. He was short, sturdy, and looked the outdoor boy. His expression was one of intense interest, as if he lived every moment of his life to its utmost, and he had the most singular eyes I ever beheld. They were very large, of a piercing light gray, and they seemed to take everything in with a kind of daring flash. Altogether, I thought, here was a lad out of the ordinary, one with latent possibilities which gave me a vague alarm.

"Wal, now, so you're Ken's brother," said Jim Williams. "I shore am glad to see you. Ken an' me was pretty tolerable pals last summer, an' I reckon you an' me kin be thet, too."

It was plain Jim liked the looks of the youngster or else he would never have made that speech. Hal approached the ranger and shook hands awkwardly. He was not timid, but backward. I saw that he was all eyes, and he looked Jim over from spurs to broadbrim with the look of one who was comparing the reality with a picture long carried in mind. Of course Ken had told Hal all about the Texan, and what that telling must have been showed plainly in the lad's manner. Manifestly he was satisfied with Jim's tall form, his sun-scorched face and hawk eyes, the big blue gun Jim packed, and the high boots and spurs he wore.

"Where's Hiram Bent?" asked Ken, earnestly.

"Hiram's back on the saddle with his hounds. He's waiting for us."

"He told me about them," replied Ken. "Lion dogs, the best in the West, Hiram said. I guess maybe I'm not aching to see them. . . . Dick! My mustang! I forgot him. What did you ever do with him? You know I left him with you at Holston last summer."

"We'll see if we can't hear something of him," I replied, evasively, as if I wanted Ken to meet a disappointment gradually. His face fell, but he did not say any more about the mustang. "Ken, I'm going to sign you into service as a ranger — my helper. Hiram is game-warden, you know, and I've arranged for us to go with him. He's specially engaged now in trying to clean out the cougars. The critters are thick as hops back on the north rim, and we've got a lively summer ahead of us."

"Sounds great," replied Ken. "Say, what do you mean by north rim?"

"It's the north rim of the Cañon — Grand Cañon — and the wildest, ruggedest country on earth."

"Oh yes, I forgot that Coconina takes in the Cañon. Will we get to see much of it?"

"Ken, in a month from now you'll be sick of climbing out of that awful gash."

For answer Ken smiled his doubts. Then, leaving Jim and Hal, who appeared to be getting on a friendly footing, I took Ken over to the office of Mr. Birch, the Supervisor of Coconina Forest Preserve. As a matter of fact, this rather superior person had always jarred on me. He was inclined to be arrogant, and few of the rangers liked him. I had to get along with him, for being head ranger, it was policy for me to keep a civil tongue in my head. When I introduced Ken and stated my desire to sign him in as my helper the Supervisor looked rebellious and said I had all the helpers I needed.

"Who is this fellow anyhow, Leslie?" he demanded. "I'm not going to have any of your Eastern friends chasing around the preserve, setting fires and killing deer. This idea of yours about a helper is only a bluff. I don't sign any more rangers. Understand?"

I bit my tongue to keep from loosing it, and while I was trying to think what was best to do Ken stepped forward.

"Mr. Supervisor," he said, blandly, "I've only come out to have a little vacation and get some practical ideas on forestry. Please be good enough to look at my credentials."

Ken handed over letters with the Washington seal stamped on them, and Birch stared. What was more when he had read the letters his manner changed very considerably, and he even looked at me with a shade of surprise.

"Oh — yes — Mr. Ward, that'll be all right. You see — I — I only — I've got to be particular about rangers and all that. Now anything I can do for you I'll be glad to do."

Ken's letters must have been pretty strong, and I was secretly pleased to see old Birch taken down a bit. The upshot of the matter was that Ken got a free hand in Coconina, to roam where he liked, and spend what time he wished with the rangers on duty. We left the office highly pleased.

"We'll go over to the corral now and look over some mustangs," I said.

From Ken's face I knew his thoughts reverted once more to the mustang which had trotted its way into his heart. But I said nothing. I wanted his surprise to be complete. Jim and Hal joined us, and together we walked down the street. Kanab was only a hamlet of a few stores, a church, a school, and cottages. My lodgings were at a cottage just at the end of the street, and here, back of a barn, was the corral. When we turned a corner of the barn there was a black mustang, all glossy as silk, with long mane flying and shiny hoofs lifting as he pranced around. He certainly looked proud. That, I felt sure, was because of the thorough currying and brushing I had given him.

Ken stopped stock-still and his eyes began to bulge. As for the mustang, he actually tried to climb over the bars. He knew Ken before Ken knew him.

"Oh! Dick Leslie!" exclaimed Ken.

Then, placing both hands on the top bar, with one splendid vault he cleared the gate.

CHAPTER II

WINGS

It did me good to see the way Ken Ward hugged that little black mustang. Somehow a ranger gets to have a warm feeling for a horse. Now, Ken's mustang remembered him, or if he did not he surely was a most deceitful bit of horse-flesh.

"He's fine and fat — in great shape," said Ken, rubbing his hands all over the mustang. "He hasn't been worked much."

"Been down on our winter range for six months," I replied. "I had him brought in this morning, and after the blacksmith clipped and shod him I took a hand myself."

"Ken, I want a mustang," sang out Hal.

He sat on the top of the corral fence, absorbed in the appearance and action of Ken's mount.

"Now, Kid, keep your shirt on," said Ken. "You'll get one. It's just half an hour since you arrived."

"That's long enough. Do you think I'm going to stand around here and watch you have a pony like that and not have one myself?"

"It's a mustang, not a pony," said Ken.

Purcell, the owner of the cottage and corrals, drove up at this juncture, and I engaged him in conversation regarding a mount for the boy and the pack-horses we would need on our trip.

"Wal, there's a bunch of mustangs over in the waterin' corral. Some good ones — all pretty wild. But about pack-hosses — that sort of bumps me," said Purcell, dubiously. "I'm due to go to Lund after grain an' supplies, an' I need my regular packers. I'll let you have one, an' the big bay stallion."

"You don't mean that big brute Marc?" I queried.

"Sure. He's all right, if you handle him easy. I don't know as he'll stand for a pack-saddle — any kind of a saddle — but you might load somethin' on him."

"If that's the best you can do we'll have to take him," I rejoined. "Also I want a good man to take care of the horses for the boys."

"Hire the Indian. He's here now, an' he's the best man to find grass an' water in this desert."

"You mean Navvy? Yes, we'd be lucky to get him, but Jim and Hiram Bent, they both hate Indians."

"Leslie, I don't know of any one else in the village. It's lambin' time now, an' hands are scarce. You'd better take the Indian, for he'll save you lots of trampin' round."

"I'll do it, Purcell. We'll pack early in the morning and get a good start. Now, take the lad over to the corral and get him a mount."

"Come on, youngster," said Purcell to Hal. "Come on an' let's see what kind of an eye you have for a hoss."

Hal leaped off the fence and went with Purcell toward the other corrals. Jim started to go with them, but Ken detained him.

"Fellows," said Ken, "before we get any farther I want to tell you about my brother. He's simply as wild as a March hare. I'm not sure, but I suspect that he's been reading a lot of Wild West stuff. The folks at home have humored him, spoiled him, I think. Father is sort of proud of Hal. The boy is bright, quick as a steel trap, and just the finest, squarest kid ever. But he has a fiendish propensity for making trouble, getting into scrapes. Now that would be bad enough back home, wouldn't it? And here I've had to bring him out West!"

"I shore am glad you fetched him," replied Jim.

"I'm glad, too, Jim, until I think of Hal's peculiarities, and then I'm scared. That kid can hatch up more impossible, never-heard-of situations than any other kid on earth. Hal imagines he can do anything. What's worse he's got the nerve to try, and, to tell you the truth, I've never yet discovered anything he couldn't do."

"Can he ride a horse?" I asked.

"Ride! Say, he can ride standing on his head. Now, Dick and Jim, I want you to do all you can to look after Hal, but understand, the responsibility for his safety and welfare doesn't rest

18

upon you. I'll do my best for him; the responsibility rests upon me. Much as I wanted Hal with me, I advised and coaxed father not to send him. But Dad thinks the kid can do anything a great deal better than I. He told me where I could go Hal could go. So we'll make up our minds to have our hearts in our throats all the time on this trip and let it go at that."

Our attention was attracted by a shout from the other corral.

"Hyar, Leslie, come over," called Purcell.

We crossed over, slipped through a couple of gates, and edging round a cloud of dust saw Hal in the middle of a corral holding a beautiful mustang by the mane.

"Leslie, the youngster has picked out Wings, the worst pinto that ever came off Buckskin Mountain," declared Purcell. "An' he says he don't want an' won't have any other mustang here."

"Sure! What did I tell you, Dick? This is where the toboggan starts. Ha! Ha!" yelled Ken.

"What's wrong, Purcell? That pinto looks fine and dandy," I said.

"He is a dandy," returned Purcell. "He's a climber, an' he can beat any hoss on the range. But he can't be rid except when he wants to be rid. There's no tellin' when he's liable to make up his mind to rare. It's not buckin' so much — he's no bronch — but he just runs wild when it pleases him, an' then it takes a Navajo to ride him. I say he's no mount for a tenderfoot."

During this speech of Purcell's I watched Hal closely, and saw that, however he occupied himself with Wings' glossy mane, he heard every word. And when he glanced up I believed that what Purcell said had absolutely decided him. The lad looked keen to me, and deep as the sea. But he was not fresh or forward, and despite my uneasiness I began to like him.

"Kid, will you take my mustang?" asked Ken.

"Nix," answered Hal. "I'm going to ride Wings and beat the life out of you and your mustang."

I sent Purcell for a saddle, and he fetched one presently and put it on Wings.

"Youngster, seein' as you are set on the pinto, all-l right," said Purcell, as he fastened the cinch.

Then Hal looked straight at the rancher.

"Mr. Purcell, I've had ponies at home and I could ride them," he said. "But this'll be new to me. Will you give me a few tips?"

That pleased me immensely. Whatever Hal was, he was not a fool. I noticed Jim Williams wore an expression as near akin to excitement as it was possible for that cool Texas ranger to wear. Perhaps in Jim's mind, as in mine, the lad was being measured. Purcell, too, appeared to like the boy's frankness.

"I don't know as I kin give you many tips," he said. "Fact of the matter is you must try to stick on, that's all. Just keep your toes in the stirrups, so you can git them out quick. Then squeeze him with your knees for all you're worth.

. . . Wait! Make sure where you're going. . . . There!"

Hal sat firmly in the saddle. Wings champed the bit and turned his head, then shook it, and suddenly lifting his hind hoofs he kicked viciously. We scattered and climbed the corral fence. When we turned round the pinto had come down on all fours and squared himself. With head down, humping his back, he proceeded to buck with startling quickness, and tossed Hal like a feather. The boy hit the ground with a thud, and slowly got up, considerably shaken. Then he went up to the mustang, now standing quietly.

Quite a little crowd of villagers, mostly boys, had collected to see the fun, and some of the latter were inclined to make remarks at Hal's expense. One of them, a boy I knew to be a rascal, poked his head between the bars of a gate, and yelled derisively at Hal, to the immense delight of the other lads. Hal eyed him a moment, but he did not say anything. This made the fellow all the bolder, for he climbed the fence, from which he directed more remarks.

"Mr. Purcell," said Hal to the rancher, "I hadn't got ready that time. I wasn't expecting it. Now how must I treat him? My way at home was to coax a pony, be decent to him."

"It'll pay best in the end to be decent to a hoss," replied Purcell. "Be kind, but firm, an' use your spurs."

"I haven't any spurs; I never used any."

"You'll need them out here."

Hal mounted the pinto again. Wings wheeled about, pranced, stood up pawing the air, snorted, and then, dropping down, he began to run round the corral. He zigzagged against the fence, and slowing down he took short jumps, kicking at the same time. Then he squared himself again and lowered his head.

"Look out, Kid!" yelled Ken.

We all shouted warnings. Hal was prepared, and for the space of a few seconds, while the bucking pinto pounded a dusty circle in the corral, he kept his seat. But a new move, a sort of sidestepping buck, flung him against the fence, and he fell all in a heap. It was a hard fall, but the boy got up. A lump began to show on his chin, and blood, his knuckles, too, were bloody.

"Lookie here, Redhead," called out the smart youngster who was amusing his comrades by making fun of Hal. "Can't you ride no better'n that? Haw! Haw! You can't ride or nothin', Redhead! Redhead!"

"Say, Johnny, can *you* ride him?" asked Hal, coolly.

"Yep, you bet."

"Come down and let me see you do it. I don't believe you."

Johnny eyed Hal rather doubtfully. Hal looked very much interested, very friendly, but his eyes were cold and hard. The Western lad hesitated, and finally driven to it by the bantering of the other lads, he dropped off the fence. Vaulting

22

into the saddle, he rode Wings round the corral, kept his seat easily while the pinto went through his tricks, and altogether gave an exhibition of riding which would have made most any Eastern lad green with envy.

"You did ride him. I was wrong. I thought you couldn't," said Hal, walking slowly up to Johnny as he dismounted. "You're a crack horseman."

Suddenly Hal leaped at the fellow, and at the same moment Ken yelled and tumbled off the fence. I was too amazed to move. Jim Williams's mouth gaped and he stared in speechless delight.

Hal had the youngster jammed against the fence and was banging him.

"You called me redhead and tenderfoot and sloppy rider!" cried Hal, swinging his fists.

Then Ken reached them, pulled Hal away, and rescued the already bewildered and bloody-nosed lad.

"Dick, I knew it, I knew it," said Ken, leading the lad out at the gate. "The minute Hal asked that boy to ride the mustang I knew what was up. I couldn't say a word. Hal always makes me speechless."

Williams was shaking so that he rattled the top bar of the corral, and Purcell roared. If it had not been for the shame and distress in Ken's face I would have yelled myself. For that bantering youngster had long ago earned my dislike, and I was glad to see him get a little of his just deserts.

Then I saw Hal look through the fence at all

the strange lads. He was certainly the coolest piece of audacity I ever saw.

"I wasn't born in a saddle, see?" he said. "At that I'll bet in a month I can ride with any of you. But there's one thing I can do right now — so don't any of you call me redhead again."

"Hal, shut up, and come out of there," called Ken.

"Not on your life," replied Hal, promptly. "I'm going to ride this iron-jawed mustang or — or —"

Hal did not complete the sentence, but his look was expressive enough.

Jim Williams leisurely dropped off the fence into the corral. While removing his spurs he looked up at Ken, and his eyes twinkled.

"See here, Ken, you're doin' a powerful lot of fussin' about this kid brother. You leave him to me."

That from Williams occasioned me immeasurable relief, and though Ken still looked doubtful there was much gladness and gratitude in his surprised glance.

Jim sauntered over toward the center of the corral, swinging his spurs.

"Kid, I reckon you an' me had better strike up a pardnership in ridin' pintoes, an' all sich little matters appertainin' to the range."

Jim changed the strap lengths on his spurs and handed them to Hal.

"Put these on," he said. "I reckon they're too long for you, an' mebbe 'll trip you up when you

24

walk. But they're what you need on horseback."

Hal adjusted the spurs, and took a few awkward steps, digging up the ground with the big rowels.

"They'll be as hard on me as on the pony," he said.

Jim captured Wings, and tightened saddle-girths, shortened stirrups, and, slipping off the bridle, let the pinto go.

"Now, kid, listen. These Western hosses an' mustangs can size up a man, an' take advantage of him. You've got to be half hoss yourself to know all their tricks. The trouble with you jest now was thet Wings seen you was scared of him. You mustn't let a hoss see that. You must be natural, easy, an' firm. You must be master. Take the bridle an' go up to Wings, on the left side. Never again try to straddle a hoss from the right side. Don't coax him, an' don't yell at him. If you say anythin', mean bizness. When you get him in a corner go right up, not too quick or too slow, an' reach out to put on the bridle as if you'd done it all your life. When you get it on draw the reins back over his head reasonable tight an' hold them with your left hand, at the same time takin' a good grip on his mane. Turn the stirrup an' slip your left toe in, grab the pommel with right hand, an' swing up. Start him off then an' let him know who's boss. If he wants to go one way make him go the other. Don't be afraid to stick the spurs into him. You're too gentle with a hoss. Thet'll never do in this country. These sage-brush hosses ain't Eastern hosses. Make up your mind to ride him now. He'll see it. An' if he bucks soak him with the spurs till he stops or throws you. An' if he throws you get up an' go after him again."

"All right," replied Hal, soberly. And picking up the bridle he went toward Wings.

The pinto squared around and eyed Hal as curiously as if he had actually heard the advice tendered by the Texan. Probably he heard the clinking spurs and knew what they meant. With a snort he jumped and began to run round the corral. Hal slowly closed in on him, and at length got him in a corner. And here Hal showed that he could obey coaching as readily as Ken. Walking directly up to the pinto, he bridled him, and with quick, decisive action leaped astride.

Then he spurred Wings. The pinto bolted, and in his plunging scattered dust and gravel. Not liking the spurs, he settled into a run. Hal was now more at ease in the saddle. It was not so much confidence as desperation. Perhaps the shortened stirrups helped him to a firmer leghold. At any rate, he rode gracefully and appeared to good advantage. He pulled Wings, and when the fiery pinto snorted and tossed his head and preferred his own way a touch of spur made him turn round. In this manner Hal ran Wings along the corral fence, across the open space, to and fro, successfully turning him at will. Then as he let up the pinto wheeled and spread his legs and tried to get his head down.

"Hold him up!" yelled Purcell.

"Now's the time, kid!" added Jim Williams. "Soak him with the spurs!"

Hal could not keep the pinto from getting his head down or from beginning to buck, but he managed to use the long spurs. That made a difference. It broke Wing's action. He did not seem to be able to get to going. He had to break and bolt, then square himself again, and try to buck.

"Stick on, Hal!" I yelled. "If you stay with him now you'll have him beat."

We all yelled, and Ken Ward danced around in great danger of being ridden down by the furious pinto. Like a burr Hal stuck on. There were moments when he wabbled in the saddle, lurched one way and then another, and again bounced high. Once we made sure it was to be a victory for the pinto, but Hal luckily and wonderfully regained his seat. And after that by degrees he appeared to get a surer, easier swing, while Wings grew tired of bucking and more tired of being spurred.

Purcell jumped into the corral and began to throw down the bars of the gate.

"Kid, run him out now!" shouted Jim. "Drive him good an' hard! Make him see who's boss!"

Wings did not want to leave the corral, and Hal, in pulling him, lifted him off his forefeet. Another touch of spurs sent the pinto through the gate. Hal spurred him down the road.

We watched Wings going faster and faster,

gradually settling into an even gait, till he was on a dead run.

"Thet pinto has wings, all right," remarked Jim. "Purcell named him some ways near right. An' between us the kid's no slouch in the saddle. He won't have thet little fire-eatin' hoss broke all in a minnit, but he'll be able to ride him. An' thet'll let us hit the trail."

CHAPTER III

OFF FOR COCONINA

The Navajo Indian whom I had engaged through Purcell did not show up till we were packing next morning. He was a copper-skinned, raven-haired, beady-eyed desert savage. When Ken and Hal had finished breakfast I called them out of the cottage to meet him.

"Here, boys, shake hands with Navvy. Here, Navvy, shake with heap big brother — heap little brother."

"Me savvy," said the Indian, extending his hand to Ken. "How."

Then he turned to Hal. "How."

Hal, following Ken, gingerly shook hands with Navvy. From the look of the lad he was all at sea, and plainly disappointed. No doubt in his mind dwelt images and fancies of picturesque plumed Indians, such as he had evolved from Western tales. Indeed Navvy would have been a disappointment to a most unromantic boy, let alone one as imaginative and full of wild ideas as Hal was. Navvy's slouch hat and torn shirt and blue jeans, some white man's cast-off apparel, were the things that disillusioned Hal. And I saw that he turned once more to his pinto. A new saddle and bridle, spurs, chaps, lasso, canteen, quirt, a rifle and a scabbard, and a slicker — these with spirited Wings were all-satisfying and gave him back his enchantment.

"Where'll the Indian ride?" asked Purcell.

"Why, he can climb on the stallion," I replied.

Purcell's stallion Marc was a magnificent bay, very heavy and big-boned. We had strapped a blanket on him and roped some sacks of oats over that. The other pack-horses were loaded with all they could carry.

"He can climb on, I reckon, but he'll darn soon git off," remarked Purcell, dryly.

"Then he'll have to walk," I rejoined.

"That'll be best," said Purcell, much relieved. "Leslie, have a care of Marc. You'll strike some all-fired bad trails in the Cañon, where many a hoss has slipped an' gone over. Don't drive Marc or pull him. Just coax him a little."

"All right, Purcell. We'll be careful. . . . Now, boys. We're late starting, and it's thirty miles to the first water."

I led the train, driving our pack horses before me. Navvy came next, leading Marc. Ken was third, and Jim, with a watchful eye on Hal and the pinto, brought up the rear.

The few miles of good road between Kanab and Fredonia, another little hamlet, we made at a jog trot, doing the distance in something over an hour. Outside of Fredonia we hit the trail,

30

and went down and down into the red washes, and over the sage speckled flats. It grew dusty and hot. About noon we reached the first slow roll of rising ridge, and from there on it was climb. More than once I looked back, and more than once I saw Hal having trouble with his pinto. Once Wings, as if he really had wings, flew off across a flat, and spilled Hal into the sage. Navvy got tired walking and climbed up on the grain-sacks on Marc, but he did not stay there very long. Then my pack horse made trouble for me by shying at a rattlesnake and getting off the trail. The time passed swiftly, as it always passed when we were on the move, and we reached the first cedars about three o'clock. Here I saw that our train was stretched out over a mile in length. Navvy was having a little ride on Marc, but Ken limped along before his mustang, and Hal changed from side to side, from leg to leg, in his saddle. The boys were beginning to show soreness from riding.

The sun had set when we made the head of Nail Gulch. Here a spring and a cabin awaited us, also a little browse for the horses.

"I've got a lame knee, all right," remarked Ken. "Thought I was in good shape."

"No matter how hard you are it'll take three days or more to break you in," I said.

Hal came straggling along behind Jim. He fell off his pinto and just flopped over against a cedar.

"Gee! but ain't it great! Ken, look at those cliffs!"

"Wait a couple of days, Hal. Then I'll show you some cliffs," I said.

It took Jim and me only a little time to unpack, build a fire in the cabin, bake biscuits, and get a good supper. Navvy led the horses to water, hobbled them and turned them loose. Then we had our meal. Ken and Hal were supremely happy, but too tired to be jolly. Darkness found them both asleep, and Hal threshed about as if he were having wild dreams.

At daybreak Navvy awakened me coming in with the horses. It began to appear that the Indian would be a welcome addition to our party. Finding the horses in the morning was work for me, and sometimes long and arduous work. And Jim, rolling out of his blanket and blinking his eyes, drawled: "Wal, pretty fair for an Injun, pretty fair!"

The boys heard us, and roused themselves, bright and eager, though so stiff they could scarcely stand erect. In an hour we had breakfasted, packed, and were in the saddle. This morning Wings did not seem to be so frisky.

"Boys, to-day will be a drill and no mistake," I told them. "Ride as long as you can stand it, then walk a bit. . . . Here! Look over the far side of the gulch. See that long black-fringed line with the patches of snow? That's Buckskin Mountain. To-night we'll camp under the pines. And Ken, there're pine-trees on Buckskin that dwarf those in Penetier."

We struck out into the trail, and then began a long, tedious, uninteresting ride. Nail Gulch was narrow, and shut in the view. Low bare stone walls and cedar slopes extended for miles and miles. It was a gradual ascent all the way, but this did not grow perceptible until about noon. I laughed to see Ken and Hal fall off their saddles, hobble along for a while, then wearily mount again, presently to repeat the performance. The air grew cooler, making gloves comfortable. About three o'clock the gulch began to lose its walls, and we reached the first pines. They were not large, and straggled over the widening gulch, but as we climbed the trail they grew more numerous. The early shades of night enveloped us as we rode out of the gulch into the level forest.

Here and there patches of snow gleamed through the gloom. This solved the question of water, and we made camp at once. A blazing fire soon warmed us. We had a hearty supper of bacon, hot biscuits, coffee, and canned vegetables. Ken and Hal were so tired and sore that they could scarcely move, but that did not affect their appetites. Then we sat around the campfire.

By this time the forest was black and the wind roared through the pines. It was not new to Ken, but Hal showed what it meant to him. I fancied him even more sensitive to impressions than Ken, but he was not so apt to express his feelings. In fact Hal seemed a silent lad, or else he had not yet found his tongue. Wonderful thoughts, I knew, were teeming in his mind. His big eyes glowed. He watched the camp-fire, and looked out into the dark gloom of the forest, and then back at Jim, then at the impassive Navajo. He listened to the wind and to the bells on the horses.

"Where's our tent?" he asked, suddenly.

"We don't use no tents," replied Jim. "We spread a tarp —"

"What's that?"

"Why, a tarpaulin, you know, a big piece of canvas. Wal, we spread one of them on the ground, roll in our blankets, an' pull the other end of the tarp up over."

Then a little while afterward Hal broke silence again.

"I hear something; what is it?" he asked, breathlessly, starting up.

We all listened while the fire sputtered. A lull came in the roar of the wind through the pines, and then from far off in the forest a wild, high-pitched yelp.

"Kid, that's a coyote," replied Ken, slapping Hal on the knee. "Don't you remember I told you about coyotes? . . . Listen!"

Hal said no more that evening, yet when I was sleepy and ready to turn in he still sat up, alert, watchful, intent on the strangeness and wildness of the forest. It was a treat to see him when Navvy rolled in a blanket with feet to the fire.

"Sleepie — me," said the Indian.

That was his good-night to us.

Ken shared my blankets and tarpaulin that night and slept without turning once. When the gray dawn came I was up lighting a fire. Jim yawned out of his bed, and both boys slept on. The morning was cold. A white frost silvered the scant grass. Presently I heard bells far off; they grew louder and quickened. Soon the horses appeared with the Navajo riding one, and they trooped into camp with thudding hoofs and jangling bells. That woke the boys.

"Rustle, now, Kid," said Jim to Hal. "You'll miss somethin' if you ain't lively."

"Oh, I'm all stove up!" exclaimed Ken. "Whew! but that's cold air! How about you, Hal?"

"I feel great," rejoined his brother. We all saw that Hal could hardly get out of bed, that when he did get out it was a desperate task for him to draw on his boots.

"Where's some water to wash in?" he asked.

"Tackle the snow-drift there."

I meant for Hal to get a pan of snow and melt it at the fire, but he misunderstood me. He tackled the snow barehanded. It had a frozen crust which he could not break through, so he kicked a hole in it, and then digging out a double handful he proceeded to wash. That operation was one which required fortitude. Hal never murmured, but he hurried to the fire in a way to make Jim wink slyly at me.

When the sun rose we were on the trail. We passed the zone of silver spruces, rode through a long aspen hollow, and then out among the brown aisles of great pines of Buckskin Forest.

"Oh! Ken, I never saw a woods before!" was Hal's tribute.

"Boys, keep your eyes peeled for deer and coyotes," I said.

It was my intention to lead Ken and Hal to the rim of the Grand Cañon without warning. I wanted the great spectacle to burst upon them unexpectedly as it had upon me. So I said nothing about it. Ken was in a dream, perhaps living over again his adventures in Penetier. Hal was suffering from his raw legs and sore joints, but he was in an ecstasy over the huge gnarled pines and the wild glades. Both boys had forgotten the Cañon. So I rode on, pleased at the thought of what it all was to them. The sun thawed the frost, letting the bluebells peep out of the grass.

"There's a black squirrel with a white tail," shouted Hal.

"Kid, don't ever yell in the forest unless it's a yelling matter," said Ken.

We flushed blue grouse in some of the hollows, but saw no sign of deer. It was easy going and we made fast time. About noon I called into requisition a little ruse I had planned to attract the attention of the boys from the trail ahead. I told them to look sharp for deer on both sides. In this way, leaving the trail and keeping behind the thicker clumps of pines, I approached the

Cañon without their suspecting its nearness. Then, rounding a thicket of juniper, within twenty yards of the rim I called out:

"Boys! Look!"

CHAPTER IV

THROUGH BUCKSKIN FOREST

Strong men, when suddenly confronted with the spectacle of the Grand Cañon, have been known to cry out in joy or fear, to weep, to fall upon their knees, or to be petrified into silence. Serious-minded men have been known to laugh immoderately. Sight of the Cañon affects no two persons alike, but there are none whom it does not affect powerfully. I paid my own moment's tribute of solemn awe, and then I glanced at the boys.

Ken looked stunned and white, his throat swelling with emotion. Hal's face shone with a radiant glow of wild joy, and for a moment he stuttered, then as Ken burst into an exclamation, he lapsed into stony silence.

"Wonderful! Beautiful! It's — it's —" That was all Ken could say.

"It shore is," replied Jim.

Then I told the boys that the Grand Cañon of Arizona was over two hundred miles long, twelve to twenty wide, and a mile and a half deep. It was a Titanic gorge in which mountains, table-lands, chasms and cliffs lay buried in purple haze, a thing of wonder and mystery, beyond any other a place to grip the heart of a man. It had the strange power to make him at once meek and then to unleash his daring spirit.

"The world's split!" exclaimed Hal. "What made this — this awful hole?"

"We'll talk of that and study it after you have seen something of its heights and depths," I replied.

At our feet yawned a blue gulf with faint tracings of cedared slope and shining cliff visible through the noonday haze. Farther out a dark-purple cañon wended its irregular ragged way to vanish in space. Still farther out rose bare peaks and domes and mesas all asleep in the sunshine. Beyond these towered a gigantic plateau, rugged and bold in outline, its granite walls gold in the sun, its forest covering a strip of fringed black. It stood aloof from the towers and escarpments, detached from the world of rock, haunting in its isolation and wild promise.

"Boys, there's the plateau, where the cougars are," I said. "You see way down to the left under the wall where a dip of ground connects the plateau to the mainland? That's the Saddle. Hiram Bent is there with his hounds waiting for us."

"How on earth will we ever get there?" queried Ken.

"There are two trails. One leads down over the rim here, the other round through the forest. We'll take the forest trail, for the lower one is not safe for you boys till you get broken in. Come now, we can make the Saddle before dark if we plug along."

With that I led off into the forest, and, what with finding the seldom-used trail, and keeping the pack-horses in it, I had no time to see how the boys fared or what they did. I knew that both were finding riding most painful, and yet were enjoying themselves hugely. It was a long roundabout way to get to the Saddle. For the most part the trail led up and down the heads of many hollows. So steep were the slopes that we had to zigzag down and up. Then the thickets of prickly-thorn and scrub-oak and black-sage were obstacles to swift traveling. One thing I discovered, and it was that the stallion Marc was the best horse I had ever seen on a trail. He would not carry the Indian, but he led the way for us and made a path through the thickets. The sun was yet an hour above the southwest rim when I reached the head of the hollow where the trail turned down to the Saddle. From a shallow ravine with grassy and thicketed slopes it deepened and widened till it was a cañon itself with looming yellow walls. It became deeper and deeper and then turning to the left it opened out into a wide space under the magnificent wall of the plateau. Here I smelled fire and presently saw the gleam of a white tent and then a column of blue smoke. The short, sharp bark of a hound rang out. I stopped and waited for Ken to catch up with me. He came along on foot, limping and leading his mustang.

"Cheer up, Ken," I said, "we're almost there."

"I'm cheerful, Dick. I'm supremely happy, but I'm all in. And as for Hal, why, Jim and I had to lift him in his saddle more times than I can remember. Dick, what're you doing to us, anyway?"

"You'll be fine in a couple of days. I wanted to get on the ground. There's Hal. Come along, Hal, you're doing well. We're almost there."

"Dick, I hear a hound," said Ken, eagerly. "Hurry up! There's smoke, too. . . . Ah! I see Hiram!"

The first sight of the old bear hunter feeding his hounds under a tree was a joy to Ken Ward. I saw it in his sparkling eyes and heard it in his exultant voice. Soon we rode through the last thicket of brush into camp. The hounds barked furiously until quieted by Hiram.

Ken, despite his crippled condition, got to the hunter in quick time, and there was a warm greeting between them.

"Youngster, the Lord is good. I hevn't been so glad about anythin' in years as I am about seein' you. . . . Wal, you have improved a heap."

Hal came forward with the same searching, luminous gaze which he had turned upon the Navajo. This time, however, the boy did not meet with disappointment. Any lad would have been fascinated with the splendid presence of the old hunter. And Hal was more than fascinated. Plain it was that Hiram's great stature, the flashing gray eyes, and the stern, weather-beaten face, his buckskin shirt, and all about him, realized the idea Hal had formed in his boyish thoughts.

"Wal, dog-gone my buttons!" said Hiram, offering an enormous hand to Hal. "Ken's brother! I've heard of you, now don't you forget thet. I'm mighty glad to meet you."

The shadow of the plateau crept out to us and shaded the camp. The sun was setting. We were down a thousand feet under the rim, so that we looked up at the plateau, and also at the peaks and towers and escarpments to the west. These were capped with pink and gold and red, and every moment the colors changed. While I was unpacking I heard Hiram ask Jim why on earth we had fetched that "tarnal redskin" with us, and Jim's reply was one that left no doubt about his idea of Indians. Both Hiram and Jim carried somewhere about in their anatomies leaden bullets which sometimes painfully reminded them that they had a grudge against Indians.

After sunset darkness settled quickly below the Cañon rim, and it was night long before we were through with supper. Then came the quiet, cheerful hour around the camp-fire, which I foresaw was to be a source of unalloyed bliss to Ken and Hal.

Hiram did not appear to be in any hurry to talk about cougars, but he was keenly interested in Ken's year at college, and especially in Ken's making the 'varsity baseball team. He asked innumerable questions, and he was delighted to learn of Ken's success and that he had been elected captain. Then he went off into reminiscences and talked of Ken's adventures in Penetier the summer before. Finally when he had satisfied his fancy he called up the hounds, one by one, and playfully, though seriously, he introduced them to the boys.

"Hyar's Prince, the best lion-hound I ever trained, bar none. He has a nose thet's perfect; he's fast an' savage, an' if ever a dog had brains it's Prince."

The great hound looked the truth of Hiram's claim. He was powerful in build, lean of loin, and long of limb, tawny-colored, and he had a noble head with great, somber eyes.

"Hyar's Curley, who's a slow trailer, an' he always bays, both fine qualities in a hound. Prince goes too swift an' saves his breath, but then it's not his fault if I don't keep close to him in a chase."

"An' hyar's Mux-Mux, who's no good."

The ugly black-and-white hound so designated wagged a stumpy tail and pawed his master, and appeared to want to make it plain that he was not so bad as all that.

"Wal, Mux, I'll take a leetle of thet back. You're good at eatin', an' then I never seen the cougar you was afraid of. An' thet's bad, fer you'll be killed some day."

"Hyar's Queen, the mother of the pups, an' she's reliable, though slow because of her lame

43

leg. Hyar's Tan, a good hound, an' this big black feller, he's Ringer. He'll be as good as Prince some day, if I can only save him."

Hiram chained each hound to near-by saplings; then lighting his pipe at the camp-fire he found a comfortable seat.

"Wal, youngsters, it's dog-gone good to see you sittin' by my camp-fire. To-morrow we'll go up on the plateau an' make a permanent camp. Thar's grass an' snow in the hollers, an' deer, an' wild hosses an' mustangs."

"Any mountain-lions, cougars?" asked Ken, intensely.

"I was comin' to them. Wal, I never in my born days seen such a network of cougars' tracks as is on thet plateau. An' at thet I've only been on one end. I'm reckonin' we'll round up the biggest den of cougars in the West. You see, no one ever hunted thet plateau but Navajos, an' they wouldn't kill a cougar. Why, a cougar is one of their gods. Wal, as I was sayin', mebbe we'll strike a whole cat tribe up thar. An', youngsters, what do you say to ketchin' 'em alive?"

"Great!" exclaimed Ken.

Hiram switched his look of inquiry to Hal. The lad's large eyes, startlingly bright, dilated and burned.

"How?" he asked, and his voice rang like a bell.

"Lasso 'em, tie 'em up," replied Hiram. Deceit could not have lived in his kindly, clear glance.

44

"Then Ken didn't lie — after all?" blurted out Hal.

"My brother never believed I helped you lasso a bear and that we intended to do the same with cougars out here," exclaimed Ken.

"It's straight goods, youngster," added Hiram. "Now, whar do you stand? Most youngsters like to shoot things. Mebbe you'd find it fun to chase cougars up trees an' then shoot 'em, but thar's a *leetle* more chance fer excitement when you pull 'em out with a rope. It keeps a feller movin' around tolerable lively. Which would you like best, then — shootin' or ketchin'?"

"I'd like best — to catch them alive," replied Hal, his voice very low.

"Wal, now, I'm glad. You see it's not the excitement I'm lookin' fer, though I ain't sayin' I don't like to rope things, but the fact is I get ten dollars for cougar skins, an' three hundred dollars for live cougars. So, you youngsters will have the fun an' I'll be makin' money, an' at the same time we'll be riddin' Coconina Preserve of bad critters. Let's roll in now, fer you're tired, an' we must be stirrin' early."

CHAPTER V

THE PLATEAU

Hiram routed us all in the morning while the shadows were still gray. There was a bustling about camp. When we were packed and mounted ready for the ascent of the plateau the pines and slopes were still shrouded in the gray gloom. Hiram led us along a trail overgrown by brush. Presently we began climbing such a steep slope that we had to hang to the pommels.

The Saddle was a narrow ridge sloping up to the plateau, and the trail zigzagged its crest. To the right a sweep of thicketed hollow led out into wide space where peaks and mesas began to show. To the left was the great abyss, filled with creamy mist. It was not possible to see a rod down toward the depths, still I had a sure sense of the presence of the Cañon. The climb was a hard task for the horses, the trail being one made by deer, but in less than an hour we were up on the rim. At that moment the sun burst out showing through rifts in rolling clouds of mist. Then we saw behind and above us the long, bold, black line of Buckskin.

Hiram took a course straight back from the rim through a magnificent forest of pines. Perhaps a couple of miles back the old hunter circled and appeared to be searching for a particular place. Presently he halted in a beautiful glade above a hollow where lay a heavy bank of snow. On the slopes the grass was yet thin, but in the glade it was thick. Here, with the snow and the grass, our problem was solved as to water and feed for the horses.

"Hyar we are," called out Hiram, cheerily. "We'll throw our camp in this glade jest out of reach of them pines on the northwest side. Sometimes a heavy wind blows one over."

We had all gotten busy at our tasks of unpacking when suddenly we were attracted by a heavy pounding on the turf.

"Hold the hosses!" yelled Hiram. "Everybody grab a hoss!"

We all made a dive among our snorting and plunging steeds.

"Youngsters, look sharp! Don't miss nothin'! Thar's a sight!" called Hiram.

The sound of pounding hoofs appeared to be coming right into camp. I saw a string of wild horses thundering by. A black stallion led them, and as he ran with splendid stride he curved his fine head backward to look at us, and whistled a wild challenge. Soon he and his band were lost in the blackness of the forest.

"The finest sight I ever saw in my life!" ejaculated Ken. "Hal, wasn't that simply grand?"

"No matter what comes off now, I'm paid for the trouble of getting here," replied Hal.

It was only a few minutes afterward that the Indian manifested excitement and pointed up the hollow. A herd of large, white-tailed deer trooped down toward us, and stopped within a hundred yards. Then they stood motionless with long ears erect.

"Shoot! Shoot!" exclaimed Navvy.

"Nary a shoot, Navvy," replied Hiram.

The Indian looked dumbfounded, and gazed from the rifles to us and then to the deer.

"Oh!" cried Hal. "They're tame deer! What beautiful, large creatures! I couldn't shoot them."

"No, youngster, they're not tame deer. They're so wild thet they aren't afraid. They've never been shot at, thet bunch. An', youngster, these deer here are mule deer an' must hev some elk in them. Thet accounts fer their big size. Now ain't they jest pretty?"

The hounds saw the herd and burst into wild clamor. That frightened the deer and they bounded off with the long, springy leaps characteristic of them.

"Look like they jump on rubber stilts," commented Hal.

"All hands now to throw camp. Fust thing, we'll pitch my tent. I tell you, youngsters, thet tent may come in right useful, if we hev a storm. An' at this altitude — we're up over seven thousand feet — we may git a snow-squall any day."

It was not long before we had a comfortable and attractive camp. At the far side of the glade stood a clump of small sapling pines in regard to which Ken said he would have to practice a little forestry. The saplings were meager and had foliage only at the top. Ken declared he would thin out that clump.

"Wal, thet's a fine idee," remarked Hiram. "Thin 'em out an' leave about a dozen saplin's each ten feet apart. They'll be jest what I want to chain our cougars to."

At that speech the faces of both boys were studies in expression. Hal, especially, looked as if he were dreaming a most wild and real adventure.

When work was finished the boys threw themselves down upon the brown pine-needle mats and indulged in rest. Hiram did not allow them much indulgence.

"Saddle up, youngsters," he called out, "Onless you're too tired to go with us."

Thereupon the boys became as animated as their aching bones and sore muscles would permit.

"Leslie, leave the Injun in camp to look after things an' we'll git the lay of the land."

"He'll eat us outen house an' home," growled Jim Williams. "I shore don't see why we fetched him, anyhow."

All the afternoon we were riding the plateau. We were completely bewildered with its impressiveness and surprised at the abundance of wild horses and mustangs, deer, coyotes, foxes, grouse and birds, and overjoyed to find innumerable lion trails. When we returned to camp I drew a rough map, which Hiram laid flat on the ground and called us around him.

"Now, youngsters, let's get our heads together."

In shape the plateau resembled the ace of clubs. The center and side wings were high and well wooded with heavy pine; the middle wing was longest, sloped west, had no pine, but a dense growth of cedar. Numerous ridges and cañons cut up this central wing. Middle Cañon, the longest and deepest, bisected the plateau, headed near camp, and ran parallel with two smaller ones, which we named Right and Left Cañons. These three were lion runways, and hundreds of deer carcasses lined the thickets. North Hollow was the only depression, as well as runway, on the northwest rim. West Point formed the extreme western cape of the plateau. To the left of West Point was a deep cut-in of the rim-wall, called the Bay. The three important cañons opened into it. From the Bay the south rim was regular and impassable all the way round to the narrow Saddle, which connected it to the mainland.

"Wal," said Hiram, "see the advantage we can git on the tarnal critters. The plateau is tolerable nigh ten miles long an' six wide at the widest. We can't git lost for very long. Thet's a big thing in our favor. We know whar cougars go over the rim an' we'll head 'em off, make short-cut chases thet I calkilate is a new one in cougar-chasin'. 'Cept whar we climbed up the Saddle cougars can't git over the second wall of rock. The first rim, I oughter told you, is mebbe a thousand feet down, with breaks in places. Then comes a long cedar an' piñon slope, weatherin' slides, broken cliffs an' crags, an' then the second wall. Now regardin' cougar sign — wal, I hardly believe the evidence of my own eyes. The plateau is virgin ground. We've stumbled on the breedin'-ground of the hundreds of cougars thet infest the north rim."

Hiram struck his huge fist into the palm of his hand. He looked at Jim and me and then at the boys. It did not take a very observing person to see that the old bear hunter was actually excited. Jim ran his hand into his hair and scratched his head, a familiar action with him when his mind was working unusually.

"We hev corraled them, shore as you're born!"

The flash in Hiram's clear eyes changed to an anxious glance, that ranged from Ken and Hal to our horses.

"I reckon some common sense an' care will make it safe for the youngsters," he said, "but some of the hosses an' some of the dogs are goin' to git hurt, mebbe killed."

More than anything else that remark, from such a man, thrilled me with its subtle suggestion. He loved horses and hounds. He saw danger ahead for them.

"Youngsters, listen," he went on, soberly. "We're in fer some chases. I want you to think first of the risk to yourselves, an' then to the hosses you ride. Don't fly often the handle. Be cool. Let your hosses pick the goin'. Keep sharp eyes peeled fer the snags on the trees, an' fer bad rocks an' places. Ken, you keep close behind Leslie as you can, an' Hal, you stick close to Jim. Course we'll lose each other an' the hounds, an' hev trouble findin' each other again. But the idee is, keep cool and go slow, when you see it ain't safe to go fast."

During supper we talked a good deal, and afterward around the camp-fire. Hal was the only one who kept silent, and he was too absorbed in what he heard to find his own voice.

But during a lull in the conversation he asked suddenly:

"I want to know why our horses carried on so this morning when that stallion ran through the woods with his band?"

"Simple enough, Hal," I replied. "They wanted to break loose and run off with the wild horses. They'll do it, too, before we leave here. We rangers have trouble keeping our horses. The mountain is overrun with mustangs and such wild bands as you saw to-day. And if we lose a horse it's almost impossible to catch him again."

Twilight descended with the shadows sweeping under the pines; the night wind rose and began its moan.

"Shore there's a scent on the wind," said Jim,

lighting his pipe with a red ember. "See how oneasy Prince is."

The hound raised his dark head, pointing his nose into the cool breeze, and he walked to and fro as if on guard for his pack. Mux-Mux ground his teeth on a bone and growled at one of the pups. Curley was asleep. Ringer watched Prince with suspicious eyes. The other hounds lay stretched before the fire.

"Wal, Prince, we ain't lookin' fer trails to-night," said Hiram. "Ken, it'll be part of your duty around camp to help me with the pack. Chain 'em up now, an' we'll go to bed."

CHAPTER VI

TRAILS

When I awakened next morning the crack of
Hiram's axe rang out sharply, and the light from
the camp-fire played on Ken's face as he lay
asleep. I saw old Mux get up and stretch himself.
A jangle of bells from the forest told me we
would not have to wait for the horses.

"The Injun's all right," I heard Hiram say.

"All rustle for breakfast," called Jim. "Ken!
. . . Hal!"

Then the boys rolled out, fresh-faced and
bright-eyed, but still stiff and lame.

"Gee! Ken, listen to the horses coming," said
Hal. "How'd Navvy ever find them? It's hardly
daylight."

"That's a secret I expect every ranger would
like to know," replied Ken.

"I like that Indian — better'n at first," went
on Hal.

We ate in the semi-darkness with the gray
shadow lifting among the trees. As we saddled
our horses dawn lightened. The pups ran to and
fro on their chains, scenting the air. The older

hounds stood quiet, waiting.

"Come, Navvy. Come chase cougie," said Hiram.

The Indian made a remarkable gesture of dislike or fear, I could not divine which.

"Let him keep camp," I suggested.

"He'll shore eat all our grub," said Jim.

"Climb up, youngsters," ordered Hiram. "An' remember all I said about bein' careful. . . . Wal, hev I got all my trappin's — rope, chains, collars, wire, nippers? Allright. Hyar, you lazy hounds — out of this. Take the lead that, Prince."

We rode abreast through the forest, and I could not help seeing the pleasure in Ken's face and the wild spirit in Hal's eyes. The hounds followed Prince at an orderly trot. We struck out of the pines at half-past five. Floating mists hid the lower end of the plateau, but cedar-trees began to show green against the soft gray of sage. The morning had a cool touch, though there was no frost. Jogging along, we had crossed Middle Cañon and were nearing the dark line of cedar forest when Hiram, who led, held up his hand in a warning check.

"Oh, Ken! look at Prince," whispered Hal to his brother.

The hound stood stiff, head well up, nose working, and hair on his back bristling. All the other hounds whined and kept close to him.

"Prince has a scent," said Hiram. "Thar's been a cougar round hyar. I never knowed Prince to

55

be fooled. The scent's in the wind. Hunt 'em up, Prince. Spread out thar, you dogs."

The pack commenced to work back and forth along the ridge. We neared a hollow where Prince barked eagerly. Curley answered, and likewise Queen. Mux's short, angry bow-wow showed that he was in line.

"Ringer's gone," shouted Jim. "He was farthest ahead. Shore he's struck a trail."

"Likely enough," replied Hiram. "But Ringer doesn't bay. . . . Thar's Prince workin' over. Look sharp, youngsters, an' be ready fer some ridin'. We're close!"

The hounds went tearing through the sage, working harder and harder, calling and answering one another, all the time getting down into the hollow. Suddenly Prince began to yelp. Like a yellow dart he shot into the cedars, running head up. Curley howled his deep, full bay and led the rest of the pack up the slope in angry clamor.

"Thar off!" yelled Hiram, spurring his big horse.

"Stay with me, Kid," shouted Jim over his shoulder to Hal. The lad's pinto leaped into quick action. They were out of sight in the cedars in less than a moment. I heard Ken close behind me, and yelled to him to come along. Crashings among the cedars ahead, thud of hoofs and yells kept me going in one direction. The fiery burst of the hounds had surprised me. Such hunting was as new to me as to the boys, and from the tingling in my veins I began to feel that it was just as exciting. I remembered that Jim had said Hiram and his charger might keep the pack in sight, but the rest of us could not.

My horse was carrying me at a fast pace on the trail of some one, and he seemed to know that by keeping in this trail part of the work of breaking through the brush was already done for him. Ken's horse thundered in my rear. The sharp cedar branches struck and stung me, and I heard them hitting Ken. We climbed a ridge, found the cedars thinning out, and then there were open patches. As we faced a slope of sage I saw Hiram on his big horse.

"Ride now, boy!" I yelled to Ken.

"I'll hang to you. Cut loose!" he shouted in reply.

We hurdled the bunches of sage, and went over the brush, rocks, and gullies at breakneck speed. I heard nothing but the wind singing in my ears. Hiram's trail, plain in the yellow ground, showed me the way. Upon entering the cedars again we lost it. I stopped my horse and checked Ken. Then I called. I heard the baying of the hounds, but no answer to my signal.

"Don't say we've lost them!" cried Ken.

"Come on! The hounds are close."

We burst through thickets, threaded the mazes of cedars, and galloped over sage flats till a signal cry, sharp to our right, turned us. I answered, and an exchange of signals led us into an open glade where we found Hiram, Jim, and Hal, but no sign of a hound.

"Hyar you are," said Hiram. "Now hold up, an' listen fer the hounds."

With the labored breathing of the horses filling our ears we could hear no other sound. Dismounting, I went aside a little way and turned my ear to the breeze.

"I hear Prince," I cried, instantly.

"Which way?" both men asked.

"West."

"Strange," said Hiram.

"Shore the hounds wouldn't split?" asked Jim.

"Prince leave thet hot trail? Not much. But he's runnin' queer this mornin'."

"There! Now listen," I put in. "There are Prince and another hound with a deep bay."

"Thet's Curley. I hear 'em now. They're runnin' to us, an' hot. We might see a cougar any minnit. Keep a tight rein, youngsters. Mind a hoss is scart to death of a cougar."

The baying came closer and closer. Our horses threw up their ears. Hal's pinto stood up and snorted. The lad handled him well. Then at a quick cry from Jim we saw Prince cross the lower end of the flat.

There was no need to spur our mounts. The lifting of bridles served, and away we raced. Prince disappeared in a trice, then Curley, Mux, and Queen broke out of the cedars in full cry. They, too, were soon out of sight.

"Hounds runnin' wild," yelled Hiram.

The onslaught of the hunter and his charger stirred a fear in me that checked admiration. I saw the green of a low cedar-tree shake and split to let in the huge, gaunt horse with rider doubled over the saddle. Then came the crash of breaking brush and pounding of hoofs from the direction the hounds had taken. We strung out in the lane Hiram left and hung low over the pommels; and though we had his trail and followed it at only half his speed, yet the tearing and whipping we got from the cedar spikes were hard enough indeed.

A hundred rods within the forest we unexpectedly came upon Hiram, dismounted, searching the ground. Mux and Curley were with him, apparently at fault. Suddenly Mux left the little glade and, with a sullen, quick bark, disappeared under the trees. Curley sat on his haunches and yelped.

"Shore somethin's wrong," said Jim, tumbling out of his saddle. "Hiram, I see a lion track."

"Here, fellows, I see one, and it's not where you're looking," I added.

"Now what do you think I'm lookin' fer if it ain't tracks?" queried Hiram. "Hyar's one cougar track, an' thar's another. Jump off, youngsters, an' git a good look at 'em. Hyar's the trail we were on, an' thar's the other, crossin' at right angles. Both are fresh, one ain't many minnits old. Prince an' Queen hev split one way, an' Mux another. Curley, wise old hound, hung fire an' waited fer me. Whar on earth is Ringer? It ain't like him to be lost when thar's doin's like this."

"What next?" asked Jim, mounting.

"I'll put Curley on the fresher trail," replied Hiram. "An' you all ought to be able to keep within hearin' of him. . . . Thar! Curley. . . . Hi! Hi!"

Curley dashed off on the trail Mux had taken. Then began some hard riding. Hal and the pinto were directly in front of me, and I saw that the lad was having the ride of his life. Sometimes he ducked the cedar branches and again he was not quick enough. There were times when I thought he would be swept from his saddle, but he hung on while the pinto made a hole in the brush. More than once Hal lost his stirrup-footing. All the time that I watched him and turned to see if Ken was all right, I was getting a thrashing from the cedars. But I felt only the severest lashes. From time to time Hiram yelled. We managed to keep within earshot of Curley, and presently reached a cañon, which, judging by depth, must have been Middle Cañon. At that point it was a barrier to our progress, but fortunately Curley did not climb the opposite slope, so we followed the rim and gained on the hound. Soon we heard Mux. Curley had caught up with him. We came to a point where the cañon was not so deep and wider, and the slopes were less rugged. Curley bayed incessantly. Mux uttered harsh howls, and both hounds in plain sight began working in a circle.

Hiram reined in his horse and leaped off, while the rest of us came to a halt.

"Off now, youngsters," said Hiram, sharply. "Tie your hosses, tight. The cougar's gone up somewhat. Run along the slope an' look sharp in every cedar an' piñon, an' in every crevice of the cliffs."

Hal jumped off, but did not tie his pinto, and he was white with excitement and panting heavily. Ken left his mustang and hurried along the ledge ahead of me. Every few steps he would stop to peer cautiously around. As if he had been struck, he suddenly straightened and his voice pealed out:

"The lion! The lion! Here he is! I see him! . . . Oh, hurry, Hal!"

I ran toward Ken, but could not see the lion. Then I stopped to watch Mux. He ran to the edge of a low wall of stone across the cañon; he looked over, and barked fiercely. When I saw him slide down a steep slope, make for the bottom of the stone wall, and jump into the branches of a cedar I knew where to look for the lion. Then I espied a round yellow ball cunningly curled up in a mass of branches. Probably the lion had leaped into the tree from the wall.

"Treed! Treed!" I yelled. "Mux has found him."

Hiram appeared, crashing down a weathered slope.

"Hyar, everybody," he bawled. "Hustle down an' make a racket. We don't want him to jump."

61

CHAPTER VII

TWO LIONS

Hiram and Jim rolled down and fairly cracked the stones in their descent. I shouted for the boys to come on. Hal never moved a muscle, and Ken seemed chained to the spot. Hiram turned and saw them.

"Ho, youngsters, are you scared?" shouted he.

"Yes, but I'm coming," replied Ken. Still he showed a strange vacillation. Overcome then by shame or anger, he plunged down the slope and did not halt till he was under the snarling lion.

"Back, Ken, back! You're too close," warned Hiram. "He might jump, an' if he does don't run, but drop flat. He's a Tom, a two-year-old, an' he's sassy."

"Don't care — whether he — jumps or not," panted Ken, bouncing about. "I've got to — be cured — of this — this —"

Whatever Ken had to be cured of he did not say, but I had no doubt that it was dread. I, myself, did not feel perfectly cool, by some dozens of degrees. The flaming eyes of the lion, his open mouth with its white fangs, his steady, hissing growls, the rippling of muscles as if it was his intention to leap at the hounds, were matters certainly not conducive to calmness.

"Will you — look at Mux!" shouted Ken.

The old hound had already climbed a third of the distance up to the lion.

"Hyar, Mux, you rascal coon-chaser!" yelled Hiram. "Out of thar!" He threw stones and sticks at the hound. Mux replied with his surly bark and steadily climbed on.

"I'll hev to pull him out, or thart'll be a dead hound in about a minnit," said Hiram. "Watch close, Jim, an' tell me if the cougar starts down. I can't see through the thick branches. He'll git mighty nervous jest before he starts."

When Hiram mounted into the first branches of the cedar Tom emitted an ominous growl, and bunched himself into a ball, trembling all over.

"Shore he's comin'," yelled Jim.

The lion, snarling viciously, started to descend, and Hiram warily backed down. It was a ticklish moment for all of us, particularly Hiram; and as for me, what with keeping an eye on the lion and watching the boys, I had enough to do. Hal's actions were singular; he would run down the slope, then run back, wave his arms and let out an Indian yell. His brother kept dodging to and fro as if he were on hot bricks. Never before had I seen such eyes as blazed in Ken Ward's face. The lion went back up the cedar, Mux climbed laboriously on, and Hiram followed.

"Fellars, mebbe he's bluffin'," said Hiram. "Let's try him out. Now all of you grab sticks an' holler an' run at the tree as if you was goin' to kill him."

The thrashing, yelling din we made under that cedar might have alarmed even an African lion. Tom shook all over, showed his white fangs, and climbed so far up that the branches he clung to swayed alarmingly.

"Here, punch Mux out," said Jim, handing up a long pole.

The old hound hung to the tree, making it difficult to dislodge him, but at length Hiram punched him off. He fell heavily, whereupon, venting his thick battle-cry, he essayed to climb again.

"You old gladiator! Git down!" protested Hiram. "What in the tarnal dickens can we do with sich a dog? Tie him up, somebody."

Jim seized Mux and made him fast to the lasso with which Curley had already been secured.

"Wal, fellers, I can't reach him hyar. I'm goin' farther up," said the hunter.

"Rustle, now," yelled Jim.

I saw that Hiram evidently had that in mind. He climbed quickly. It was enough to make even a man catch his breath to watch him, and I heard Ken gasping. Hiram reached the middle fork of the cedar, stood erect and extended the noose of his lasso on the point of his pole. Tom, with a hiss and a snap, savagely struck at it. A second trial tempted the lion to seize the rope with his teeth. In a flash Hiram withdrew the pole and lifted a loop of the slack noose over the lion's ears. The other end of the lasso he threw down to Jim.

"Pull!" he yelled.

Jim threw all his weight into action, pulling the lion out with a crash, and giving the cedar such a tremendous shake that Hiram lost his footing. Grasping at branches and failing to hold, he fell, apparently right upon the lion. A whirling cloud of dust arose, out of which Hiram made prodigious leaps.

"Look out!" he bawled.

His actions, without words, would have been electrifying enough. As I ran to one side the lion just missed Hiram. Then with a spring that sent the stones rattling he made at Ken. The lad dove straight downhill into a thicket. When the furious lion turned on Jim, that worthy dropped the lasso and made tracks. Here the quick-witted Hiram seized the free end of the trailing lasso and tied it to a sapling. Then the wrestling lion disappeared in a thick cloud of dust.

"Dod gast the luck!" yelled Hiram, picking up Jim's lasso. "I didn't mean for you to pull him out of the tree. He'll kill himself now or git loose."

When the dust cleared away I discovered our prize stretched out at full length, frothing at the mouth. As Hiram approached, swinging the other lasso, the lion began a series of evolutions that made him resemble a wheel of yellow fur and dust. Then came a thud and he lay inert.

Hiram pounced upon him and loosened the lasso round his neck.

"I'm afraid he's done fer. But mebbe not. They're hard-lived critters. He's breathin' yet. Hyar, Leslie, help me tie his paws together. . . . Be watchful."

As I came up the lion stirred and raised his head. Hiram ran the loop of the second lasso round the two hind paws and stretched Tom out. While in this helpless position, with no strength and scarcely any breath, he was easy to handle. With Jim and me attending strictly to orders Hiram clipped the sharp claws, tied the four paws together, took off the neck lasso and substituted a collar and chain.

"Let him breathe a little. He's comin' round all right," said Hiram. "But we're lucky. Jim, never pull another cougar clear out of a tree. Pull him off over a limb an' hang him thar while some one below ropes his hind paws. Thet's the only way, an' if we don't stick to it somebody'll git chewed up."

Ken appeared, all scratched and torn from his header into the thorny brake. As he gazed at our captive he whooped for Hal. The lad edged down the slope and approached us eagerly. He was absolutely unconscious that we were laughing at him. His face was in a flush, with brow moist and his telltale eyes protruding. Whatever the few thrilling moments had been to us, they must have been tame compared to what they had been to Hal.

"Wal, youngster, whar were you when it came off?" inquired Hiram, with a smile.

"Have we got him — really?" whispered Hal.

"Shore, Kid. He's a good cougar now," answered Jim.

"Come along an' watch me put on his muzzle," said Hiram.

Hiram's method of performing this part of his work was the most hazardous of all. He thrust a stick between Tom's open jaws, and when the lion crushed it into splinters he tried another and yet another, till he found one that did not break. Then, while Tom bit on it, Hiram placed a wire loop over the animal's nose, slowly tightening it till the stick would not slip forward of the great canine teeth.

"Thar, thet's one, ready to pack to camp. We'll leave him hyar an' hunt up Prince an' Queen. They've treed the other cougar by this time."

When Jim untied Mux and Curley it was remarkable to see what little interest they had in the now helpless lion. Mux growled, then followed Curley up the slope. We all climbed out and mounted our horses.

"Hear thet!" yelled Hiram. "Thar's Prince yelpin'. Hi! Hi! Hi!"

From the cedars across the ridge rang a thrilling chorus of bays. Hiram spurred his horse and we fell in behind him at a gallop. We leveled a lane of sage in that short race, and when Hiram leaped off at the edge of the impenetrable cedar forest we were close at his heels. He disappeared and Jim and Ken followed him. I heard them smashing the dead wood, and soon a deep yell mingled with shouts and the yelps of the hounds. I waited to tie Ken's mustang, and I had to perform a like office for Hal, whose hands trembled so he could not do it. He jerked his rifle out of his scabbard.

"No, no, Hal, you won't want that. Put it back. You might shoot somebody in the excitement. Come on. Keep your wits. You can climb or dodge as well as I."

Then I dragged him into the gloomy clump of cedars whence came the uproar. First I saw Ken in a tree, climbing fast; then Mux in another, and under him the other hounds with noses skyward; and last, up in the dead topmost branches, a big tawny lion.

"Whoop!" the yell leaped past my lips. Quiet Jim was yelling; Ken was splitting the air, and Hiram let out from his cavernous chest a booming roar that almost crowned ours.

I lifted and shoved Hal into a cedar, and then turned to the grim business of the moment. Hiram's first move was to pull Mux out of the tree.

"Hyar, Leslie, grab him; he's stronger'n a hoss."

If Mux had been only a little stronger he would have broken away from me. Jim ran a rope under the collar of all the hounds; there both of us pulled them from under the lion.

"It's got to be a slip-knot," said Jim, as we fumbled with the rope. "Shore if the cougar jumps we want to be able to free the hounds quick."

Then while Hiram climbed Jim and I waited. I saw Ken in the top of a cedar on a level with the lion. Hal hugged a branch and strained his gaze, and, judging from the look of him, his heart was in his throat. Hiram's gray hat went pushing up between the dead snags, then his burly shoulders. The quivering muscles of the lion grew tense, and his lithe body crouched low. He was about to jump. His dripping jaws, his wild eyes roving for some means of escape, his tufted tail swinging against the twigs and breaking them, manifested his terror and extremity. The hunter climbed on with a rope between his teeth and a long stick in his hand.

"Git ropes ready down thar!" yelled Hiram.

My rope was new and bothersome to handle. When I got it right with a noose ready I heard a cracking of branches. Looking up, I saw the lion biting hard at a rope which circled his neck. Jim ran directly under the tree with a spread noose in his hands. Then Hiram pulled and pulled, but the lion held firmly. Whereupon Hiram threw his end of the rope down to me.

"Thar, Leslie, lend a hand."

We both pulled with might and main; still the lion was too strong. Suddenly the branch broke, letting the lion fall, kicking frantically with all four paws. Jim grasped one of the lower paws and dexterously left the noose fast on it. But only by a hair's breadth did he dodge the other whipping paw.

"Let go, Leslie," yelled Hiram.

I complied, and the rope Hiram and I had held flew up over the branches as the lion fell, and then it dropped to the ground. Hiram, plunging out of the tree, made a flying snatch for the rope, got it and held fast.

"Stretch him out, Jim," roared Hiram. "An' Leslie, stand ready to put another rope on."

The action had been fast, but it was slow to what then began. It appeared impossible for two strong men, one of them a giant, to straighten out that wrestling lion. The dust flew, the sticks snapped, the gravel pattered against the cedars. Jim went to his knees, and Hiram's huge bulk bowed under the strain. Then Jim plowed the ground flat on his stomach. I ran to his assistance and took the rope which he now held by only one hand. He got up and together we lent our efforts, getting in a strong haul on the lion. Short as that moment was it enabled Hiram to make his lasso fast to a cedar. The three of us then stretched the beast from tree to tree, after which Hiram put a third lasso on the front paws.

"A whoppin' female," said Hiram, as our captive lay helpless with swelling sides and blazing eyes. "She's nearly eight feet from tip to tip, but not extra heavy. Females never git fat. Hand me another rope."

With four lassoes in position to suit Hiram the lioness could not move. Then he proceeded to tie her paws, clip her claws, muzzle and chain her.

"I reckon you squirrels can come down now," remarked Hiram, dryly, to the brothers. "See hyar, one of these days when we git split, thar'll be mebbe no one to help me but one of you youngsters. What then?"

To Hal and Ken, who had dropped out of their perches, the old hunter's speech evidently suggested something at once frightful and enthralling.

"Shore as you're born thet's goin' to happen," added Jim, as he wiped the sweat and dust from his face.

"I never felt — so — before in my life," said Hal, tremulously. "My whole insides went like a crazy clock when you break a spring. . . . Then I froze — scared stiff!"

His naïve confession strengthened any already favorable impression.

Ken laughed. "Kid, didn't I say it was coming to you?"

Hal did not reply to this; he had shifted his attention to the hounds. Jim was loosing them from the rope. They had ceased yelping and I was curious to know how they would regard our captive.

Prince walked within three feet of the lioness, disdaining to notice her at all, and lay down. Curley wagged his tail; Queen began to lick her sore foot; Tan wearily stretched himself for a nap; only Mux, the incorrigible, retained antipathy for our bound captive, and he growled once low and deep, and rolled his bloodshot eyes at her as if to remind her it was he who had brought her to such a pass. And, on the instant, Ringer, lame and dusty from travel, trotted into the glade, and, looking at the lioness, he gave one disgusted grunt and flopped down.

CHAPTER VIII

IN CAMP

How should we get our captives to camp? This was the task which we faced next. We sent Ken back for the pack-horses. He was absent a long while, and when at length he hove in sight on the sage flat it was plain that we were in for trouble. Marc, the bay stallion, was on the rampage.

"Why didn't he fetch the Injun?" growled Hiram, who lost his temper only when things went wrong with the horses. "Spread out, boys, an' head him off."

We managed to surround the stallion and Hiram succeeded in getting a halter on him. Ken's face was red, his hair damp, and he looked as if he had spent an hour or two of trying responsibility.

"I didn't want the bay," he explained. "But I couldn't drive the others without him. And what do you think of this? When I told the Indian that we had two lions he ran off into the woods. Say! maybe I haven't had some bother with that stallion. I think riding him will be the only way to get him anywhere. That's what I'm going to do next time."

"Wal, first thing when we get to camp I'll scalp the redskin," said Jim.

"Youngster, you needn't be so flustrated," put in Hiram. "I reckon you did well to git Marc hyar at all."

As they talked they were standing on the open ridge at the entrance to the thick cedar forest. The two lions lay just within the shade. Hiram and Jim, using a pole, had carried our first captive, whom we had named Tom, up from the cañon to where we had tied the lioness.

Ken, as directed, had brought a pack-saddle and two long canvas sacks. When Hiram tried to lead the horse that carried these, the animal began to tremble and pull back.

"Somebody unbuckle the straps," yelled Hiram.

It was good luck that I got the sacks and saddle off, for in three jumps the horse broke from Hiram and plunged away across the sage flat.

"Shore he'll belong to the band of wild hosses," commented Jim.

I led up another horse and endeavored to hold him while Jim and Hiram got the pack-saddle on. It would have taken all three of us to hold him.

"They smell the lions," said Hiram. "I was afraid they would. Consarn the luck! Never had but one nag thet would pack lions."

"Try the sorrel," I suggested. "He looks amiable."

For the first time in a serviceable life, according to Hiram, the sorrel broke his halter and kicked like a plantation mule.

"Shore they're scared," said Jim. "Marc ain't afraid. Try him."

Hiram gazed at Jim as if he had not heard aright.

"Go ahead, Hiram, try the stallion," I added. "I like the way he looks."

"Pack cougars on thet hoss!" exclaimed the astounded Hiram.

"Shore," replied Jim.

The big stallion looked a King of horses — just what he would have been if Purcell had not taken him when a colt from his wild desert brothers. He scented the lions, for he held his proud head up, his ears erect, and his lame dark eyes shone like fire.

"I'll try to lead him in an' let him see the cougars. We can't fool him," said Hiram.

Marc showed no hesitation, nor indeed anything we expected. He stood stiff-legged before the lions and looked as if he wanted to fight.

"Shore he'll pack them," declared Jim.

The pack-saddle being strapped on and the sacks hooked to the horns, Hiram and Jim, while I held the stallion, lifted Tom and shoved him down into the left sack. A madder lion than Tom never lived. It was hard enough to be lassoed and disgrace enough to be "hog-tied," as Jim put it, but to be thrust down into a bag and packed on a horse was more than any self-respecting lion could stand. Tom frothed at the mouth and seemed like a fizzing torpedo about to explode. The lioness, being considerably larger, was with difficulty gotten into the other sack, and her head and paws hung out.

"I look to see Marc bolt over the rim," said Hiram. "An' I promised Purcell to hev a care of this hoss."

Hiram's anxiety clouded his judgment, for he was wrong. Marc packed the lions to camp in short order, and as Jim said, "without turnin' a hair." We saw the Navajo's head protruding from behind a tree.

"Here, Navvy," I called.

Hiram and Jim yelled derisively, whereupon the black head vanished and did not reappear. Then they unhooked one of the sacks and dumped out the lioness. Hiram fastened her chain to a small pine-tree, and as she lay powerless he pulled out the stick back of her canines. This let the wire muzzle fall off. She welcomed so much freedom with a roar. The last action in releasing her from the bonds Hiram performed with much dexterity. He slipped the loop fastening one paw, which loosened the rope, and in a twinkling let her work the other paws free. Up she sprang, mouth wide, ears flat, and eyes ablaze.

Before the men lowered Tom from the pack-saddle I stepped closer and put my face within six inches of his. He promptly spat at me. I wanted to see the eyes of a wild lion at close range. They were beautiful. Great half-globes of tawny amber, streaked with delicate lines of black, surrounded pupils of purple fire.

"Boys, come here," I called to Ken and Hal. "Don't miss this chance. Bend close to the lion and look into his eyes."

Both boys jerked back as Tom spat and hissed, but presently they steeled their nerves and got close enough.

"There. . . . What do you see?"

"Pictures!" exclaimed Ken.

"I want to let him go free," replied Hal, instantly.

It pleased me that the brothers saw in the eyes of the lion much the same that I had seen.

Pictures shone there and faded in the amber light — the shaggy-tipped plateau, the dark pines and smoky cañons, the yellow cliffs and crags. Deep in these live pupils, changing, quickening with a thousand vibrations, quivered the soul of this savage beast, the wildest of all wild nature, unquenchable love of life and freedom and flame of defiance and hate.

Hiram disposed of Tom in the same manner he had the lioness, chaining him to an adjoining small pine, where he leaped and wrestled.

"Dick, look! There comes Jim with Navvy," said Ken.

I saw Jim leading and dragging the Indian into camp. I felt sorry for Navvy, for I believed that

77

his fear was not so much physical as spiritual. The lion, being a Navajo god, was an object of reverence to the Indian, and it seemed no wonder that Navvy hung back from the sacrilegious treatment of his god. Forced along by Jim, the Navajo dragged his feet and held his face sidewise. Jim drew him within fifteen feet and there held him, while Hiram tried to show and tell the poor fellow that the lions would not hurt him. Navvy stared and muttered to himself. Jim seemed to have some deviltry in mind, for he edged up closer, but just then Hiram pointed to the loose horses and said to the Indian:

"Chineago" (feed).

But no sooner had Jim released Navvy than he bolted, and the yells sent after him made him run only the faster.

"He'll come back when he gits hungry," said Hiram. "Ken, you drive the hosses down in the holler whar thar's good browse."

With an agile leap Ken swung up on the broad back of the stallion.

"Hyar, youngster, pile off thar!" called Hiram. "Wal, dog-gone me!"

It appeared that our great stallion had laid aside his noble disposition and was his old self once more. Before Ken had fairly gotten astride Marc dropped his head, humped his shoulders, brought his feet together and began to buck. It looked to me as if Marc was a tougher bucking proposition than the wildest broncho that ever romped the desert. For Marc was unusually robust and heavy, yet exceedingly active. I had seen him roll over in the dust three times each way and do it easily, something I had never seen equaled by another horse.

Ken began to bounce. He twisted his strong hands in the mane of the stallion and held on. It was plain that Ken's blood was up. And all of us, seeing that it was now safer for him to keep his seat, began to give encouragement.

"Shore you're doin' fine," yelled Jim. But I fancied that Jim did not mean Ken was really doing well. Hiram's concern changed to mirth and he roared. It was as funny to see Hal as it was to see Ken. The younger lad was beside himself with excitement and glee. He ran around Marc and his shrill yells pealed out.

"Stay with him, Ken. . . . Stick on. . . . Hug him tight. . . . Get a new hold. . . . Look out!"

Then Marc became a demon. He plowed the ground. Apparently he bucked five feet straight up. Before Ken had bounced. Now he began to shoot up into the air. But the lad was powerful and his hold did not break easily. Higher and higher he rose, and then the last time his heels went over his head. He went up to the full extent of his arms, and when he came down heavily his hold broke. He spun around on the broad back of the stallion and went hurtling to the ground. The soft pine-needle mat saved him from injury and he sat up. "Jiminy!" he exclaimed, "no wonder Navvy didn't ride him."

When we recovered from our mirth Jim drawled out:

"Ken, thet was the best buckin' I ever seen a hoss do. Shore Marc could buck off a cinched saddle."

"Ken, I reckon you'll hev to knuckle to Marc," said Hiram, "an' you better ride your own hoss."

"Don't worry," replied Ken. "I know when I have got enough." He mounted his mustang and drove Marc and the other horses down into the hollow. When he returned we all saw Navvy sneaking into camp behind him. The Indian stopped at a near-by pine, but seeing that we appeared not to be concerned about him, he presently approached.

We all busied ourselves with camp-fire tasks, and I helped Ken feed the hounds. To feed ordinary dogs is a matter of throwing them a few bones; our dogs, however, were not ordinary. It took time to feed them and a prodigious amount of meat. We had packed a quantity of wild-horse meat which had been cut into small pieces and strung on the branches of a scrub-oak.

Prince had to be fed by hand. I heard Hiram say the hound would have starved if the meat had been thrown indiscriminately to the pack. Curley asserted his rights and preferred large portions at a time. Queen begged with solemn eyes, but for all her gentleness she could eat more than her share. Tan needed watching, and Ringer, because of imperfectly developed teeth, had to have his portion cut into small pieces. As for Mux-Mux — well, great dogs have their faults — he never got enough meat. He would fight poor crippled Queen, and steal even from the pups, and when he had gotten all that Ken would give him and all he could snatch, he would waddle away with bulging sides, looking like an old Dutch man-of-war.

"Will our lions eat?" asked Hal.

"Not for days," replied Hiram. "Mebbe we can tempt them to eat fresh rabbits in a week or so. But they'll drink to-night."

We made a hearty meal, and afterward Hiram and Ken and I walked through the woods toward the rim. A yellow promontory, huge and glistening, invited us westward, and after a detour of half a mile we reached it. The points of the rim, stretching out into the immense void, always drew me irresistibly. We found the view from this rock one of startling splendor. The corrugated rim-wall of the middle wing extended to the west, and at this moment apparently reached into the setting sun. The golden light, flashing from the millions of facets of chiseled stone, created color and brilliance too glorious and intense for the gaze of men. And looking downward was like looking into the placid, blue, bottomless depths of the Pacific.

"Here, help me push off this stone," I said. We heaved on a huge round stone, and were encouraged to feel it move. Fortunately we had a little slope; the boulder groaned, rocked and began to slide. Just as it toppled over I glanced at the second-hand of my watch. Then with eyes over the rim we waited. The silence was the silence of the cañon, dead and vast, intensified by our breathless ear-strain. Ten long, palpitating seconds and no sound! I gave up. The distance was too great for sound to reach us. Fifteen seconds — seventeen — eighteen —

With that a puff of air seemed to rise, bringing a deafening peal of thunder. It rolled up and widened, deadened, to burst out and roll louder, then slowly, like mountains on wheels, rumbled under the rim-walls, passing on and on, to roar back in echo from the cliffs of the mesas. Roar and rumble — roar and rumble! For two long moments the dull and hollow echoes rolled at us, slowly to die away at the last in the far-distant cañons.

"Thet's a mighty deep hole," commented Hiram.

Twilight stole upon us idling there, silent, content to watch the red glow pass away from the buttes and peaks, the color deepening downward to meet the ebon shades of night creeping up like a dark tide.

On turning toward camp we tried a short cut, which brought us to a deep hollow with stony walls. It seemed better to go around it. The hollow, however, was quite long, and we decided presently to cross it. We had descended a little way when suddenly the old hunter held me back with his big arm.

"Listen," he whispered.

It was quiet in the woods; only a faint breeze stirred the pine-needles; and the weird, gray darkness seemed approaching under the trees.

I heard the patter of light, hard hoofs on the scaly sides of the hollow.

"Deer?" I asked, in a low voice.

"Yes; see," he replied, pointing ahead, "jest under thet broken wall of rock; right thar on this side; they're goin' down."

I descried gray objects, the color of the rock, moving down like shadows.

"Have they scented us?"

"Hardly; the breeze is against us. Mebbe they heerd us break a twig. They've stopped, but are not lookin' our way. Wal, I wonder —"

Suddenly there was a rattle of stones, followed by an indistinct thud as from the impact of soft, heavy bodies, and then the sound of a struggle in the hollow.

"Lion jumped a deer," yelled Hiram. "Right under our eyes. Come on! Ken, pull your gun on the critter. Thar he goes! Hi! Hi! Hi!"

Hiram ran down the incline, yelling all the way, and I kept close to him. Toward the bottom, the thicket barred our progress, so that we had to smash through. But Ken distanced us. His yell pealed out and then *Crack! Crack!* went his six-shooter. I saw a gray, swiftly bounding object too long and too low for a deer. Hurriedly drawing my revolver I worked the trigger as fast as I could. Ken also was shooting, and the reports blended in a roar that echoed from the cliff. But for all our shots the cougar got away.

"Come here — this way — hurry," called Ken.

Hiram and I crashed out of the brush, and in another moment were bending over a gray mass huddled at Ken's feet. It was a deer, gasping and choking.

"A yearlin' doe," said Hiram. "Look hyar, low down on her neck, whar the tarnal cat bit in. Hear thet wheeze? Thet's blood in her throat. Ken, if you hev another shot put her out of pain."

But neither Ken nor I had an extra cartridge about us, nor did Hiram have his clasp knife, and we had to stand there silent until the doe quivered and died.

Then a signal cry rang down the slope.

"Thet's Jim," said Hiram. "It didn't take him long to git to us."

There was a crashing of brush, quick thud of flying feet, and Jim loomed up through the gathering darkness. He carried a rifle in each hand, and he moved so assuredly and looked so formidable in the dusk that I thought of what such a reinforcement would mean at a time of real peril.

"Jim, I've lived to see many strange happenin's," saw Hiram, "but this was the first time I ever seen a cougar jump a deer."

"Shore you did enough shootin' to make me think somethin' had come off," replied Jim.

We soon returned to camp the richer by a quantity of fresh venison.

Hal was sitting close to the fire and looked rather white. I observed that he had his rifle. He did not speak a word till Ken told of our little adventure.

"Just before all the yells and shots I happened to be watching Prince," said Hal. "He was uneasy; he wouldn't lie down; he sniffed the wind and growled. I thought there must be a lion about."

"Wal, I shore wish Ken had plugged him," said Jim.

I believed Jim's wish found an echo in all our hearts. At any rate, to hear him and Hiram express regret over the death of the doe justified in some degree my own feelings. The tragedy we had all but interrupted occurred every night, perhaps often in the day, and likely at different points at the same time. Hiram told how he had found fourteen piles of bleached bones and dried hair in the thickets of less than a mile of the hollow on which we were encamped.

"We'll rope the danged cats, boys, or by George! we'll kill them! Wal, it's blowin' cold. Hey, Navvy, coco! coco!"

The Indian, carefully laying aside his cigarette, kicked up the fire and threw on more wood.

"Discass" (cold), he said to Ken; "coco weyno" (fire good).

Ken replied, "Me savvy — yes."

"Sleep-ie?" he asked.

"Moocha," returned Ken.

While we carried on a sort of novel conversa-

85

tion, full of Navajo, English, Spanish, and ges-
tures, absolute darkness settled down upon us.
I saw the stars disappear. The wind, changing
to the north, grew colder, and carried a breath
of snow. I liked a north wind best — from under
the warm blankets — because of the roar and
lull and lull and roar in the pines. Crawling into
bed presently I lay there and listened to the rising
storm-wind for a long time. Sometimes it swelled
and crashed like the sound of a breaker on the
beach, but mostly, from a low, incessant moan,
it rose and filled to a mighty rush, then suddenly
lulled; and this lull was conducive to sleep.

CHAPTER IX

A VISIT FROM RANGERS

The Navajo awoke us with his singing. Ken peeped lazily from under the blankets and then covered himself again. The air was cold and flakes of white drifted through our wind-break of pine boughs.

"Snow!" exclaimed Ken.

"By all that's lucky," I replied. "Hiram wants snow more than anything."

"Why?" queried Ken.

"So we can track lions. Also have plenty of snow-water. Roll out now, Ken."

"Oh-h-h! but I'm sore," groaned Ken, as he laboriously got up and began to pull on his boots. "Baseball training isn't one — two — six to this work."

"Stay off bucking horses," I replied.

We walked to a roaring camp-fire. The others were all astir, even Hal being up and busy. Hiram's biscuits, well browned and of generous size, had just been dumped into the middle of our tarpaulin table-cloth; the coffeepot steamed fragrantly and a huge skillet sizzled with a quantity of sliced venison.

"Youngster, did you hear the Injun?" asked Hiram, as he poked red coals in a heap round the skillet.

"His singing woke me," answered Ken.

"It wasn't a song. Thet's the Navajo's mornin' prayer, a chant. Wal —"

Growls and snarls from the lions interrupted him. I looked up to see Hal fooling round our captives. They were wet, dirty, bedraggled. Hiram had cut down a small pine and made shelters for the lions, but they did not seem disposed to keep out of the snow.

"Let 'em alone, youngster," said Hiram to Hal. "They won't be drove. Mebbe they'll git in out of the wet arter a while. . . . We're havin' good luck an' bad. Snow's what we want. But now we can't git the trail of the lion thet killed the doe."

"Chineago!" called Jim, who like the rest of us had begun to assimilate a little of the Navajo language.

Whereupon we fell to eating with appetites unknown to any save hunters. Somehow the Indian gravitated to Hal at meal-times, and now he sat cross-legged beside him, holding out a plate and looking as hungry as Mux. At the first he always asked for what happened to be on Hal's plate, and when that became empty he gave up imitation and asked for anything he could get. The Navajo had a marvelous appetite. He liked sweet things, sugar best of all. It was a fatal error to let him get his hands on a can of fruit. Although he inspired Hiram with disgust and Jim with worse, he was a source of unfailing pleasure to the boys.

"What's on for to-day?" queried Ken.

"Wal, we may as well hang round camp an' rest the hounds," replied Hiram. "I intended to go after the lion thet killed the deer, but this snow has taken away the scent."

"Shore it'll stop snowin' soon," said Jim.

The falling snow had thinned out, and looked like flying powder; the leaden clouds, rolling close to the tree-tops, grew brighter and brighter; bits of azure sky shone through rifts.

Navvy had tramped off to find the horses, and not long after his departure we heard the jangle of bells. Then he appeared, riding Hal's mustang, and racing the others toward camp.

Ken and I set to work building a shack for the hounds. And when we finished it there was no need of it, for that time at least, because all the snow had gone. The sun was shining warmly and the forest was as brown and almost as dry as on the day before.

"Wal, it's a good idee to hev a day of rest onct in a while," said Hiram, in answer to Ken's impatient desire to be on the hunt. "Youngster, you'll git all you want. But I tell you it might be useful fer us to prowl round an' explore some of these hollers. We'll need to know all about 'em, places to cross, whar they head, an' sich as thet. Now you an' Dick go north, an' Jim an' me'll go south. Hal can keep camp with Navvy."

So Ken and I started off on foot. We found the hollows extremely interesting. They began where the forest of pines merged on the sage flats. Some were shallow and some deep V-shaped cuts, too steep for us to go straight down. The thickets of scrub-oak lined the slope and thickets of aspen covered the bottom. Every hollow had its well-defined deer and lion trail, and every thicket its grisly heap of bones and hide. We jumped deer and flushed grouse, and out of one hollow we chased the wild stallion and his band. Ken was delighted at the sight of them. After several hours of leisurely exploring we returned toward camp.

"Dick, I see strange horses," said Ken, as we drew near.

Sure enough, there were horses in camp that did not belong to our party, and presently I saw men who were not Hiram or Jim. We had visitors.

"Perhaps they're some Mormon wild-horse hunters," I replied. "I hope so, for I'd like you to meet some of those fellows, and go on a hunt with them. . . . No, they're rangers. Now, Ken, I don't like this for a cent."

As we walked into camp neither Hal nor the Indian was in sight. Three rangers lolled about under the pines. One of them I did not know; the others had worked with me and did not like me any better than I liked them, which was not much. Then a fourth fellow appeared from somewhere in the shade, and when I recognized him I was divided between anger and distrust at this invasion of our camp. This fourth individual, Belden by name, had been a ranger, and as he had been worthless, and a hindrance to other rangers, I got his discharge. It had been an object of worry to me that after his discharge he still remained on the preserve. In fact all these men were Mormons, and they resented the advent of Hiram, Jim, and myself. The bone of contention was that the forest department had put us over them. And the hard feelings had been shared even by the forest supervisor, who was strongly in sympathy with native rangers. To me the present situation looked as if these men had been sent to spy on us, or they had undertaken that on their own account.

"Hello, fellows," I said, "what are you doing out here? Thought you were building a cabin at Quaking-Asp."

"We're jest pokin' around," replied one, a man named Sells, and he was the best of the lot.

"We want to see how you trap them cougars," said another.

Belden laughed loudly. "An' me, I'm sort of scouting around, too, Leslie; I've got a new job."

"With the forest service?" I queried.

"Yep."

"What kind of a job?"

"I'm keepin' tab on all the rangers. The Supervisor says it'll go hard with any ranger ketched with fresh venison."

Belden looked meaningly at me. I thought the fellow was lying about a new job, still I could not be certain as to that. But there was no doubt about the gleam in his eyes meaning that he had caught me breaking the law.

"Belden, we've got fresh venison in camp — but we didn't kill it."

"Haw! Haw! Haw!" he guffawed.

It was hard for me to keep my temper. On the moment I was glad to see Hiram and Jim approaching. Hiram stopped near where the lions were chained and I heard him mutter: "Wal, what in the tarnal dickens is the matter with thet lion?" From where I stood I could not see either of our captives. Jim lounged into camp, and as he glanced with keen eyes from our visitors to me his genial smile faded.

"Shore we've got company," he drawled.

I would have replied in no cordial acknowledgment of the fact, but just then Hal came out of the tent, and sight of him cut short my speech. Hal wore a broad red mark across his cheek, and any one could have seen that it was a mark made by a blow. Moreover, he trembled either with excitement or anger, and on closer view I saw that under his tan he was pale.

"Hal!" exclaimed Ken, sharply. "What's the matter with you?"

"Nothing. I'm all right."

"That's not so. I'd know from the look of you, without that red welt on your face. Who hit you?

Hal — you couldn't have gotten in a scrap with Navvy?"

"Nope — never mind how I got the welt. I got it and that's enough," replied Hal.

Where Hal got that mark did not appear any great mystery to me. I would have staked my horse that Belden had given the blow.

"Sells," I demanded, "which one of you struck the lad?"

Sells removed his pipe and puffed a cloud of smoke. He did not seem in any hurry to reply.

"Speak up, man. Who hit the lad — Belden, wasn't it?"

This time the ranger nodded.

"What for? What did he do? . . . Haven't you a tongue? Talk! I want to know —"

I felt Ken Ward's hand on my arm and I hesitated. He took one long step forward.

"This boy is my brother," he said. "Do I understand you to mean one of you hit him?"

Again Sells nodded.

"Which one of you?" added Ken.

Sells pointed to the grinning Belden. Ken made a quick, passionate movement, and took another long step that seemed involuntary; then he wheeled to his brother.

"Hal, what have you done this time? You promised me you'd behave if I brought you out West. I declare I'm ashamed of you. I'll never —"

"Cheese it! Shut up!" cried Hal, hotly. "You're always blaming me. How do you know I deserved getting slapped? Do I always deserve the worst of everything?"

"Nearly always, Hal, I'm sorry to say," returned Ken, gravely.

"Well, this is one of the few times when I don't, then," said Hal, sullenly.

"What did you do?" demanded Ken.

"I called that fellow every name I could lay tongue to," retorted Hal, pointing a quivering finger at Belden. "I called him a liar and a coward. Then he hit me."

"Why did you call him names?"

"He saw the deer meat hanging there on the tree and he kept saying we shot the deer. But I held my temper. Then he got to teasing Tom and trying to hold him with a forked stick. He said we caught the lion in a trap and he was looking for trap-marks. Tom batted him one, scratching him a little. Then he took up a club —"

At this juncture Hiram Bent strode into the circle and he roared: "Who clubbed thet lion? If the Injun —"

The old hunter was angry clear through.

"Hold on, Hiram," I interrupted. "We're getting at the thing. Hal was just telling us. Go on, lad."

"Look here, Hal," spoke up Ken, in great earnestness, "tell the absolute truth. Don't stretch. Give me your word. Then I'll believe you, and if I do, so will Hiram and Dick and Jim."

Hal repeated precisely what he had told us before Hiram's interruption, and then he went on: "Belden took up a club and beat Tom over the head — beat him till I was sure Tom was dead. Then I couldn't stand it longer, so I called Belden a brute, a coward, a liar — everything I could think of. So he hit me, knocked me down, and kicked me."

"Leslie — the youngster's tellin' it straight," said Hiram. "Thet cougar is all bunged up, an' any sneak who would beat a chained animal would hit a boy."

The old hunter then turned to Belden. That worthy had ceased to grin. I looked closely at him to see if he had been drinking, but it was not that; he was surely sober enough.

"Belden, afore I say anythin' else I'd like to know what you mean by carryin' on this way," went on Hiram. "Mebbe you think beatin' up chained cougars an' boys as are keepin' camp ain't serious. Wal, I reckon you'll change your idee."

"Bent, I'd change no idees of mine," rejoined Belden. "An' one idea I got is then you trapped them cougars. An' another idee is thet I ketched you killin' deer. An' thet's agin the law. I'm agoin' to put you through for it."

For answer Hiram strode to a pine-tree some twenty paces from his tent and took down something from a dead snag. As he returned I saw it was the head and neck of the yearling doe. He showed it to Belden, and pointed out the laceration made by the teeth of the lion. Belden did not speak. Then Hiram showed the wound to the other rangers.

"Sells, you're a woodsman. Now what made thet wound?"

"A cougar killed thet doe an' no mistake," admitted Sells.

"Thar!" The old hunter threw down the deer head and whirled to face Belden. I never saw a man any more furious than Hiram was, holding himself in control.

"I ain't carin' a tarnal flip what sich as you think of my capturin' cougars. But fer beatin' up a helpless animal I care this much — you're wuss than the youngster called you — you're the wust dog I ever seen. An' fer hittin' this youngster I'm goin' to pay you back in —"

Ken Ward caught the old hunter's arm. The boy was white, but he was as cool as ice, and his eyes had the dark flash I had once or twice before seen in them. He stepped in front of Hiram and faced Belden.

"Belden, I'll give you a chance to beat me up."

"Hey?" queried Belden in stupid surprise.

Hiram and Jim appeared too amazed for speech; and as for me I saw with a kind of warm thrill what was coming off.

"Hey?" mocked Ken. "What do you think? I mean fight."

Belden kept on staring. He was a grown man and probably could not conceive the idea of a boy wanting to fight him. But I knew Ken Ward, and I saw, too, that he was nearly as big as Belden, and when I compared the two and thought of Ken's wonderful agility and strength I felt the call of battle rise within me. Then conscience troubling me, I made a half-hearted attempt to draw Ken back. I was too late. The lad reached out with his hand — his powerful right hand that had acquired much of its strength in gripping baseballs — and he seized Belden's nose between his fingers. It was no wonder he did it. Belden's nose was long and red, an offensive kind of nose. The effect was startling. Like a mad bull Belden roared. Ken pulled him round, this way and that, then he let go and squared himself. Bellowing furiously, the ranger rushed at Ken. The lad appeared to step aside and flash into swift forward action at the same instant. A sharp thud rang out and Belden stopped in his rush and staggered. But he did not fall.

Then Ken began to dance around the ranger. Any fight always roused me to a high pitch of excitement, and this one gripped me so intensely that I could scarcely see it. But then Ken Ward was so swift in action that even in a calm moment it would not have been easy to follow his motions. I saw enough to know that the fight he had made with the Greaser when I was bound fast was as nothing to this one. Ken appeared to be on all sides of Belden at once. He seemed to have as many arms as a centipede has legs.

Belden's wildly swinging fists hit the air. The way his head jerked up showed the way Ken was hitting, and the sound of his blows rang out like rapid pistol-shots. Belden's swarthy face grew red and swollen. All at once I seemed to hear mingled yells from Hiram and Jim, and that made me conscious that I was yelling myself. Ken's gray form flashed around Belden and the rain of scientific blows went on. Suddenly Ken stepped back and swung heavily. Belden went to his knees, staggered up, only to be met with a stunning shock that laid him flat.

He stirred laboriously, groaned and cursed, tried to sit up and fell back. He was bloody; his nose looked like a red cauliflower; one eye was nearly closed. Ken stood erect panting hard, still flaming-eyed, still unsatisfied. His face showed a few marks of conflict.

Hiram Bent looked down at Belden.

"Dog-gone it! You did git a tarnal good lickin'! . . . Hey?"

This good-humored query from the lately furious Hiram brought the rest of us to our senses.

CHAPTER X

HAL

Presently Belden got to his feet. He did not look at Ken or any of us, and went directly for his horses. He saddled and packed with hurried hands. It showed what the humiliation meant to him as well as what kind of a fellow he was that he rode away without a word to his companions.

They were disposed to make a joke of it and were not above praising Ken. Soon afterward they put up a tent and began preparations for supper. I certainly had no desire for their company, but neither had I any right to ask them to move on, so I thought it was just as well that we should try to be friendly.

"If you all don't mind we want to see you ketch a cougar," said Sells.

"Sartinly — glad to show you," replied Hiram.

And shortly we were laughing and talking around the camp-fire just as if there had not been any unpleasantness. I noticed, however, that Hal did not speak a word to any of our visitors, and indeed he was uncivil enough not to reply to questions they put. This gave me the idea that Hal had not told all of what had been done to him during our absence. Certainly he was not the kind of a boy to blab things. From the light in his big gray eyes I fancied that he was cherishing a righteous anger against these invaders. I made a note, too, of how intently he listened to all they said.

"Look a-here, Bent," Sells was asking, "is there any danger of them cougars gittin' loose?"

"Wal, sometimes they break a collar or chain. I lose probably one out of ten thet way. But I can't tie them up any tighter, for they'd choke themselves to death."

"Durn me if I like to sleep so close to cougars as this," went on Sells. "I allus wus scared of 'em; jest can't stand fer cats, any kind, nohow."

"Nother am I powerful enraptured at the idee," remarked one of his companions.

"Then why did you throw up the tent so close to them?" demanded Sells.

"Nary danger, fellers," put in Hiram. "My cougars won't hurt you onless you git in their way. Then I reckon you'd git a swipe."

We talked and smoked around the camp fire for an hour or more. Then the north wind rose, roaring in the pines, and the night air grew cold. Soon we all sought our blankets.

I quickly dropped off to sleep. Sooner or later after that I was awakened by a terrible sound. Sitting up with a violent start I felt Ken's hands clasping me like a vise. I heard his voice but could not distinguish what he said. For the uproar in the camp made hearing anything else impossible. Blood-curdling shrieks, yells and curses mingled with sounds of conflict. They all came from the rangers' tent. By the pale moonlight I saw the tent wavering and shaking. Then followed the shrill rending of canvas. Hiram emerged from the gloom and bounded forward. I jumped up eager to help, but ignorant of what to do, I held back. Then bang, bang, bang, went a revolver, and bullets whistled about.

"Lay low!" roared Hiram, above the tumult in the tent.

Promptly I pulled Ken with me behind a pine and peeped forth.

To make the din worse all the hounds began to bark furiously. Suddenly there came a violent shock from a heavy body plunging against the inside of the tent. It waved this way and that, then collapsed. From the agitated canvas came hoarse, smothered bellows. If I had not been so nonplussed I would have given up to laughter. But something was terribly wrong with the rangers. I saw a dark form roll from under the tent, rise and flee into the forest. Then another emerged from the other side. The yells ceased now, to be followed by loud cries of some one in pain.

With this Hiram ran forward. I saw him bend over, and then was astounded to see him straighten up and begin to haul away on something. But a gray, bounding object explained the mystery. Hiram was dragging one of the cougars back from the demolished tent.

"By George! Ken, one of the lions got loose," I exclaimed, "and it must have run right into the rangers' tent."

"Great!" replied Ken Ward.

I jumped up and ran to help Hiram, but he had the cougar tied when I got to him. Even in the excitement I noticed that he was untying a lasso from the end of the chain. I looked at Hiram and he looked at me.

"Don't say nothin'," he whispered. "Somebody tied this rope in the chain, then pulled the cougar over to the rangers' tent. I found the lasso tied to the tent-stake."

"Whew! What's come off?" I ejaculated. "Who did it?"

"How on earth he did it I can't reckon, but I'll bet it was thet tarnal boy."

"Hal? . . . Impossible, Hiram!"

"Wal, I reckon there ain't much thet's impossible fer Ken Ward's brother. . . . Come on — somebody's hurt — we can figure it out afterward."

Jim appeared, and then two men emerged from the dark shadow of pines. One was Sells. Little was said on the moment. We lifted the tent and underneath we found the other ranger. If he had been as badly hurt as he was frightened I thought surely we would presently have a dead ranger on our hands. It turned out, however, that when we washed the blood from his face we found he had been badly scratched but not seriously injured. And as neither Sells nor the other ranger had been hurt the tension of the moment lessened, and Hiram particularly appeared greatly relieved.

"I woke up," said Sells, "an' seen thet durned cougar jump right in the tent. He was quicker'n lightnin' an' he began to leap at me. I dodged him, an' yellin' like mad I tried to git out. But every time I got near the tent door the cougar made at me an' I hed to dodge. Then he got us all goin', an' there was no chanct to do anythin' but roll over an' jump an' duck. Pell throwed his gun an' begin to shoot, an' if the tent hedn't fallen in he'd plugged one of us. . . . I jest knowed one of them cougars would rustle us last night."

Plain it was that Sells had no suspicion of a trick. This relieved me. I glanced round for Hal, but he was not in sight and I supposed he had not rolled out of his blankets. Presently all was quiet again in camp, except that the lions were restless and clanked their chains. Sells and his companions had moved away some distance under the pines. Before I went to sleep again I told Ken what Hiram had said about Hal, and Ken replied: "Oh yes! I knew whatever it was Hal did it!"

"But Jim must have had a hand in it," I declared. "How could Hal drag the lion, even if he had the nerve?"

"Dick, that boy could drag a rhinoceros around if by it he could get even with somebody

who had mistreated him. You take my word —
those rangers did something to Hal more than
we know."

"Well, whatever they did to him he's square
with them. Did you ever hear such yelling? They
were scared wild."

"Reminds me of the time Greaser and Herky-
Jerky got mixed up with my bear-cub in the old
cabin on Penetier. Only this was worse."

We soon slept again, and owing to the break
in our slumbers did not awaken until rather late.
Sells and his rangers had decided they did not
care so much after all to see Hiram tie up a lion,
and with the rising of the sun they had departed.

"Shore it's good riddance," declared Jim.

"Where's Hal?" asked Ken.

His question acquainted me with the fact
that Hal was missing. At once Ken appeared
troubled.

"Don't worry, youngster," assured Hiram.
"Your brother will turn up presently."

"Have you seen him this morning?"

"Nary a hair of him," replied Hiram.

"Have you, Jim?"

"I shore hevn't. An' what's more he wasn't in
bed when I got rustled out last night by thet
infernal racket. An' he didn't come back."

"Wal, now, thet's new on me," said Hiram,
getting serious.

Ken began to pace up and down before the
camp-fire. "If anything happens to Hal how can
I ever face my father again?"

"See hyar, youngster. I reckon your father is a sensible man," rejoined Hiram. "He knowed things was goin' to happen to thet wild kid, an' thet's why he sent him with you. Hal will get his eye teeth cut out hyar. I calkilate it'll be wise fer you to jest stop worryin', an' let things happen."

"Shore, shore," added Jim, earnestly.

"There's a good deal of sense in what Hiram says," I said. "No doubt Hal is hiding somewhere. And he'll come in as soon as he finds out the rangers have gone. . . . Jim, weren't you in that trick last night?"

"I shore wasn't," replied Jim, complacently. I knew then that it would be impossible ever to find out whether or not he had really aided Hal.

"Hiram, would it have been possible for Hal to pull off that lion stunt all by himself?" I inquired.

The old hunter looked thoughtful.

"Wal, it does seem onreasonable. But I ain't doubtin' it. The youngster is strong an' a daredevil. Then he has watched me handlin' the cougars. He's a wonder on imitation, thet boy. It's a fact thet a young cougar, arter he's been tied up fer a day or so, will be kinder sluggish fer a little on bein' dragged round agin. He'll hang back, an' not begin to jump an' pull an' fight till he's waked up thoroughly. It's quite possible, I reckon, thet Hal sneaked up to the tree, loosed the chain an' tied a rope to it. Then he dragged the cougar over to the rangers' tent, tied the rope to the tent-stake, an' then — wal, I'm balked. How did he git the cougar into thet tent? He'll hev to tell us."

"It's a wonder no one was killed," said Ken.

"It shore is," replied Jim.

"I wish he'd come in," went on Ken. "Only — what'll he do next?"

We got breakfast, ate it, and still Hal did not put in appearance. The Navajo came in, however, and that made us wonder how far he had been from the camp. Jim was of the opinion that Navvy had been so scared by the uproar that he had run till he dropped. I observed pine-needles thick in Navvy's black hair, and knew he had slept somewhere under a pine.

Hiram went to feed the hounds and almost instantly I heard him exclaim: "Wal, I'll be dog-goned!"

"What's the matter, Hiram?"

"The pup's gone, too. He didn't break away. He's been untied, that's sartin. Fer I was pertickler to fasten him tight. He's been crazy to run off an' trail somethin'. The youngster he's took him."

Ken marched over to where Hal kept his saddle and outfit. "He left his rifle and all the rest of his trappings."

A sudden thought made me grow cold. "Hiram, mightn't Sells have fooled us? Pretended he didn't know the trick, and then got hold of Hal? . . . Those Mormons wouldn't think much of dropping him over the rim."

"Oh! no!" cried Ken Ward.

Following that we all fell silent, and instinctively looked to the old hunter for help or assurance. But Hiram appeared much disturbed in mind. All at once a little shock went over his tall form, making him suddenly rigid.

"Listen!" he said.

I complied with all my ears, but heard nothing except the wind in the pines and the hammering of a flicker on a dead branch.

"Shore —" began Jim.

Hiram held up a finger in warning.

"Listen — with the puffs of wind."

Then followed a long listening silence. After what seemed an age I heard a faint yelp of a hound. It was so low that it was almost indistinguishable. Jim heard it, too, and at last Ken, as I could tell by their faces. We all remained silent, still held by Hiram's uplifted finger.

"It's the pup," said Hiram, finally. "He's way over to the west. I reckon he's arter a coyote — or else he's yelpin' because somethin's happened to — Now, fellers, I'll make a bee-line fer whar I think he is. If I let out a string of yells you all come a-runnin' with dogs an' guns. If I yell onct head me off to your left. If twice, head me off to your right."

With that he took up a rifle and strode rapidly off into the forest. Jim had nothing to say, and I did not look at Ken, for from Hiram's unfinished speech it looked as if he feared an accident had befallen Hal.

We waited moments and moments. Once Ken imagined he heard a shout, and then Jim turned a doubtful ear to the west, but I assured them they were mistaken. Presently we were electrified by rapid yells far off in the forest, yet clear and ringing on the wind. Jim unchained the hounds and strung a rope through their collars while Ken and I gathered up guns and ropes. The Navajo was as excited as we were, and he followed us out of camp, but soon lagged behind. We ran across the level glades and through the brown aisles, and up and down the hollows.

Jim called a halt and pealed out a signal to Hiram. The answer came and again we ran. The hounds had become excited by this unusual proceeding; they barked and plunged to get away from Jim. Ken distanced us, and Jim yelled for him to wait. When we caught up with him once more Jim sent out a cry. This time Hiram's answer proved we were traveling off to the right, so we sheered round and hurried on. Openings in the green-black wall of pines showed me that we were nearing the rim. The hollows grew deeper and had to be headed, which change of direction threw us out of line.

Jim's next signal drew a stentorian blast from the old hunter, and that caused us to run with all we had left in us. Then at the end of a long aisle we saw Hiram waving to us and we had a mad race that Ken won by several rods.

I stopped, panting for breath, and surveyed the glade with quick eyes. At the same moment the pack of hounds burst into wild clamor.

"There's Hal!" shouted Ken, in a glad voice. I saw the lost lad sitting composedly on a log. Next I saw the pup. He was quite beside himself, yelping, leaping, and his nose pointed straight upward. Following the direction thus indicated I looked up in a short dead pine-tree to see a snarling lion.

CHAPTER XI

HIRAM CALLS ON KEN

The full wild chorus of the hounds mingled with our yells of exultation. Prince stood on his hind legs and pawed the air in his eagerness to get to the lion. Mux-Mux, the old war-dog, had as usual lost his reason.

When we had calmed down somewhat Hiram said: "It's another two-year-old, an' fair-sized. Fellars, thet's the best tree fer our ropin' purposes I ever seen a cougar in. Spread out now an' surround him, an' keep lively an' noisy."

When Hiram swung himself on the first stubby branch of the pine, the lion, some fifteen feet above, leaped to another limb, and the one he had left cracked, swayed, and broke. It fell directly upon Hiram, the blunt end striking his head and knocking him out of the tree. Fortunately, he landed on his feet; otherwise there would surely have been bones broken. He appeared stunned, and reeled so that Jim caught him. The blood poured from a wound in his head.

This sudden shock sobered us instantly. On examination we found a long, jagged cut in Hiram's scalp. We bathed it with water from my canteen and with snow Jim procured from a near-by hollow, eventually stopping the bleeding. I insisted on Hiram coming to camp to have the wound properly dressed, and he insisted on having it bound with a bandanna.

"I reckon it doesn't amount to much," said Hiram. "But I'm a little dizzy, an' better not climb any more. . . . Wal, youngster, hyar's whar I call on you."

He directed this last remark toward Ken.

"What — what?" stammered Ken.

"I want you to go up an' slip the rope over the cougar's head. We'll do the rest."

Ken's face went first red, then white. He gave a kind of eager gasp and a wild start at once. He stared at the old hunter and it was a full moment before his natural color returned.

"You want — me to rope him?"

"Sartinly. You are supple an' quick, an' with me to tell you what to do, the job can be done better'n if I went up arter him. Don't be scared now, Ken. If he gits sassy up thar I'll warn you in plenty of time."

Without a word Ken took the lasso and began to climb the pine. Hal Ward stood as if petrified; only his eyes seemed alive, and they were wonderful to behold. I appreciated what the situation meant to the boy — he had not believed Ken's stories of an old hunter roping wild beasts, and

111

here was Ken himself about to perform the miracle!

"Not so fast, youngster," called Hiram. "Don't crowd him. It's hard to tell what move he'll make next, an' thar's the danger." The cougar changed his position, growled, spat, clawed the twigs, and kept the tree-trunk between him and Ken.

"Wait — he's too close to the tree," said Hiram. "You've got to chase him out on a limb. It'll be best for you to git a little above him, Ken. Try an' scare him. Break off a branch an' throw at him."

Ken was eighteen feet below the cougar, on the opposite side of the tree. He broke off a snag and thrashed and pounded; then throwing it he hit the beast square in the side. There was an explosion of spits and snarls and hisses.

"Thet's the way," yelled Hiram. "Make him think you're goin' to kill him. Go on up now, hurry! Don't hesitate. He'll back out on thet thick branch."

It surely must have tried Ken's nerve to obey the hunter. I thought that Ken could have been excused if he had not obeyed. But he climbed on and slowly the cougar backed out on the limb.

"Shore, Ken, you're more at home in thet tree than the critter himself," cried Jim.

And so it really appeared, for Ken's movements were rapid and certain, his lithe, powerful form seemed to glide up between the branches without effort, and the lion was awkward and slow, plainly showing he feared he might fall.

"Thar, Ken, thet'll do," shouted Hiram, as Ken reached a point a little above the cougar. "Now you're right. Make a noose, not too big, an' sort of pitch it. . . . Try again, youngster, an' be deliberate. You're nervous. You're perfectly safe, 'cause if he gits a notion to start fer you jest climb up farther. He'll never foller you up. . . . Thar! . . . You ketched him thet time. Whoop!"

We all whooped, and I thought Jim Williams would stand on his head. He had come to exhibit the most extraordinary delight in the achievements of the lads.

"Draw the noose tight. . . . Jest pull easy-like, fer he's bitin' at the rope, an' if you jerk too hard you'll — Thar! I could hev done no better myself. Come down now. . . . No, don't climb down. Slide down on the rope."

Ken had not spoken a word since he had gone up the pine, and now he turned his tense white face down to us, and looked as if he had not heard aright.

"Slide down the rope," yelled Hiram. "It'll hold."

With that Ken gave the lasso a strong pull and the lion braced himself. Then Ken stepped off the limb and slid down the lasso, hand over hand, while the lion held his weight with apparent ease. Ken was breathing hard and he had the expression of a man whom strong, thrilling excitement had carried through a deed the reality of which he scarcely appreciated.

"Make your noose ready," yelled Hiram to Jim.

I had dropped my rope to help them pull the animal from his perch. The branches broke in a shower; then the lion, hissing, snarling, whirling, plunged down. He nearly jerked the rope out of our hands, but we lowered him and then Hiram noosed his hind paws in a flash.

"Make fast your rope," shouted he. "Thar, thet's good! Now let him down — easy."

As soon as the lion touched ground we let go the lasso, which whipped up and over the branch. He became a round, yellow, rapidly moving ball. Jim was the first to catch the loose lasso and he checked the rolling cougar. Hiram leaped to assist him and the two of them straightened out the struggling animal, while I swung another noose. On the second throw I caught a front paw.

"Pull hard! Stretch her out!" yelled Hiram. He grasped up a stout piece of wood and pushed it at the lion. He caught it in his mouth, making the splinters fly. Hiram shoved the head of the beast back on the ground and pressed his brawny knee on the bar of wood.

"The collar! The collar! Quick!" he called.

I threw the chain and collar to him, which in a moment he had buckled on.

"Thar, we've got him!" he said. "It's only a short way over to camp, so we'll drag him without muzzlin'."

As he rose the lion lurched, and, reaching for him, fastened its fangs in his leg. Hiram roared. Jim and I yelled. And Ken, though frightened, was so obsessed with the idea of getting a picture that he began to fumble with the shutter of his camera.

"Grab the chain! Pull him off!" bawled Hiram.

I ran in and took up the chain with both hands, and tugged with all my might. Jim, too, had all his weight on a lasso. Between the two of us we choked the hold of the lion loose, but he tore Hiram's leather legging. Then I dropped the chain and jumped.

"Hyar! Hyar!" exploded Hiram to Ken. "Do you think more of a picture than savin' my life?" Having expressed this not unreasonable protest, he untied the lasso that Jim had made fast to a small sapling.

Then we three men, forming points of a triangle around an animated center, began a march through the forest that for variety of action and uproar beat any show I ever saw.

So rare was it that the Navajo came out of hiding and, straightway forgetting his reverence and fear, began to execute a ghost dance, or war dance, or at any rate some kind of an Indian dance, along the side lines.

There were moments when the lion had Jim and me on the ground and Hiram wobbling; others when he ran on his bound legs and chased the two in front and dragged the one behind; others when he came within an ace of getting his teeth into somebody.

We had caught a tartar. We dared not let him go, and though Hiram evidently ordered it, no one made his rope fast to a tree. There was no chance. The lion was in the air three parts of the time and the fourth he was invisible in dust. The lassos were each thirty feet long, but even with that we could just barely keep out of reach.

Then came the climax, as it always comes in a lion hunt, unexpectedly and with lightning swiftness. We were nearing the bottom of the second hollow, well spread out, lassos taut, facing one another. I stumbled and the lion leaped. The weight of both brought Jim over, sliding and slipping, with his rope slackening. The leap of the lion carried him within reach of Hiram; and as he raised himself the cougar reached a big paw for him just as Jim threw all his strength and bulk on his lasso.

The seat of Hiram's trousers came away with the claws of the lion. Then he fell backward, overcome by Jim's desperate lunge. Hiram sprang up with the velocity of an Arab tumbler, and his scarlet face, working spasmodically, and his moving lips, showed how utterly unable he was to give expression to his rage. I had a stitch in my side that nearly killed me, but laugh I would if I died for it.

But it was no laughing matter for Hiram. He volleyed and thundered at us.

All the while, however, we had been running from the lion, which brought us, before we realized it, right into camp. Our captive lions cut up fearfully at the hubbub, and the horses stampeded in terror.

"Whoa!" yelled Hiram, whether to us or the struggling cougar no one knew. But Navvy thought Hiram addressed the cougar.

"Whoa!" repeated Navvy. "No savvy whoa! No savvy whoa!" which proved conclusively that the Navajo had understanding as well as wit.

Soon we had another captive safely chained and growling away in tune with the others. I went back to untie the hounds, to find them sulky and out of sorts from being so unceremoniously treated. They noisily trailed the lion into camp, where, finding him chained, they gave up in disgust.

Hiram soon recovered from his anger and laughed loud and long at what he considered the most disgraceful trick he had ever had played on him by a cougar.

Then as we sat in the shade resting, well content with ourselves, Hiram and Jim and Ken began to fire questions at Hal. The lad was, as usual, not inclined to talk. But the old hunter's admiration and Jim Williams' persuasive questions at length proved too much for Hal. His story of getting the lion to the tent of the rangers tallied precisely with the manner in which Hiram had explained it.

"Wal, I reckoned on thet," said Hiram. "But, youngster, how did you ever git the lion inside the rangers' tent? Thet stumps me."

Hal appeared surprised.

"Why, I didn't put the lion in the tent. And the lion didn't go in the tent. When I tied the lasso to the tent-stake Tom began to wake up and buck. He lunged back near the door of the tent and began to roar and spit. Just then I guess Sells woke up and began to bawl. I crawled away and got behind a tree. Then I watched. It looked to me as if the rangers just got up and ran here and there with the tent over them. Gee! but didn't they howl. But I know positively that the lion was not in the tent at all."

"How on earth did that ranger get all scratched up?" I asked.

" 'Peared to me them scratches were sorter unlike cougar scratches," remarked Hiram. "Thet fellar scratched himself wrastlin' round."

"Shore, then, thet story of Sells was a big yarn. Why, the way he talked you'd thought the tent was full of cougars," said Jim.

"I reckon Sells lied, but he believed what he said. Probably he waked up an' seein' the cougar between the flaps of the tent he was so scared thet he imagined all the rest. An' of course his yellin' thet way was enough to scare the other rangers into fits. Why, I was scared myself."

We had a good laugh at the expense of Sells and his companions, and our conviction was that they had paid dearly for their spying visit.

"Wal, *then* what did you do?" went on Hiram.

"I untied one of the hounds, the first I got my hands on," replied Hal. "I wanted to go off in the woods, because I thought the rangers would find out I put up the job on them. And I wanted company, so I took the dog. I sat up awhile and then fell asleep. When I awoke the woods were getting gray. It was near daylight. The pup had left me, and presently I heard him barking way off in the woods. I went after him and when I found him he had the lion treed. That's all."

"Oh, that's all, eh?" inquired Ken, with a queer look at his brother. "Well, I hope it holds you for a while."

"Youngster, I can't find the heart to scold you now," said Hiram, soberly. "But you was careless of yourself an' the feelin's of others."

"Shore, kid, you was plumb bad," added Jim. "As it turned out thet lion stunt tickled me most to death. It shore did. But mebbe the luck of it was accident. Don't pull off no more tricks like thet."

I added my advice to that of the others, but I observed that Hal, though he appeared contrite and subdued, did not make any rash promise as to future behavior.

CHAPTER XII

NAVVY'S WATERLOO

That night we were sitting around the campfire, and Hiram was puffing at his pipe in a way that seemed rather favorable for the telling of a story he had long promised the boys.

It was an unusually cool night, so cool that we all hugged the fire except Hal. He hung back in the shadow. This action I would scarcely have noted particularly had he not made elaborate efforts to attract attention to some real or pretended task. I had come to regard Hal with considerable doubt, and felt safer to watch him from a distance.

Navvy sat right upon the fire, stolid as usual, with his bright black eyes fixed upon the red embers. From time to time he puffed at a cigarette. Ken had a seat back of the Indian, just out of the severest heat, and he left it occasionally to stir and rake some coals over a potato he was baking.

"It's shore fine round the camp-fire," remarked Jim, spreading his hands to the blaze.

"Thar's snow in the wind," said Hiram. "It reminds me —"

Just then Ken poked the embers again. Startling as a flash of lightning the camp-fire blew up in a blinding flare. It burst into a huge light, and exploded with a boom into millions of sparks. Pieces of burning wood flew every way. Red embers and hot ashes and showers of sparks covered us. I heard the Indian yell, and Ken yelled still louder. Then came black darkness.

We were all threshing about, scared out of our wits, and trying to beat the fire from our burning clothes. That was a pretty lively moment. When the excitement quieted down a little I heard Jim's wrathful voice. Hiram was so astounded he could not be angry.

"Dog-gone me!" he ejaculated. "What in the tarnal dickens was thet? Youngster, was thet a potato you was bakin' or a dinnamite bomb?"

"By George!" declared Ken, breathing hard. "You've got one on me! I've no idea what happened. Make a light. I'm burned alive."

It developed presently, when Hiram got a fire blazing some yards distant from the dangerous camp-fire site, that Ken had been pretty severely burned. His face was black with charcoal. It took several moments for us to put out the burning holes in his shirt and trousers. Ken's hands trembled, and when he washed the black from his face we saw that he was pale. He had been badly frightened, but fortunately had escaped serious injury.

For a little while we all talked at once so that I could hardly grasp anything we said. The Indian came warily out of the darkness, and this was the first we had seen of him since the explosion. We had forgotten all about him. He had been sitting near the fire, but, though apparently more frightened than Ken, he had not been so badly burned.

"Hey! Hal, where are you?" called Ken.

"Here," came a response from the wood-pile.

"Are you all right?"

"Sure. Never touched me," replied Hal.

"Scared you though, I'll bet."

"It'd take more than a busting log of fire-wood to scare me."

Ken was silent. We were all silent, revolving Hal's cool explanation of the explosion.

"Oh-h — it would!" finally exclaimed Ken, and there was a world of meaning in his peculiar tone of voice.

Hiram growled low and deep. Jim was shaking in silent mirth. And the Navajo was staring from one to the other of us, as if he did not know what to make of such company. He kept feeling his shirt, and this action led me to the discovery that his shirt was wet. Not only was it wet, but hot.

"Hiram, the Indian's shirt is all wet, and mighty hot, too," I said. "Did you have a pot of water on the fire? It might have tipped and caused the blow-up."

It was plain from the fact that Hiram did not trust his memory, and went to look over his outfit of pans and pots, that he was much disturbed in mind.

"Mebbe — mebbe," he said, as he fumbled among them. "Dog-gone it! — no! Hyar they all are, an' nary one wet."

"Jim, can you smell powder?" I asked.

"No. Thet shore must have been a bustin' log," replied Jim.

"That was a steam explosion, my man," I replied. "Somebody put a sealed fruit-can in the fire, or buried a jar of water in the ashes."

No more was said on the moment, but later, when Hal and Jim were tying up the dogs, Ken broke out emphatically:

"Another job of the kid's! Whatever it was it certainly got me. I was never so scared in my life. Hiram, isn't there any way we can scare Hal? It's got to be done."

"Wal, youngster, I'll think on it."

"Let's play a trick on Hal, give him a dose of his own medicine. Hiram, it's a wonder to me he hasn't done something to you and Dick. He will yet."

"Wal, youngster, I reckon you'll find Leslie an' me accomplices in any reasonable trick on thet thar lad."

"It'll be great. . . . But what he'll do to us, if he ever finds it out, will be a-plenty."

By this time Ken seemed obsessed with his idea, yet all the while he showed a strange half-reluctance, as if he bore in mind Hal's remarkable powers of retaliation.

"But how?" he asked. "Can we coax Jim into the scheme?"

"Leave that to me, Ken," I said. "Jim would fall victim to any fun. Now, we'll get Jim to fire Hal out of his bed, and we'll all refuse to take him in ours on some pretext or other. Then the Navajo will naturally gravitate to Hal, and we'll find some way to scare him."

Next morning I found a favorable opportunity, wherein I approached Jim with my proposition and won him over easily. He had weakness of that sort.

We hunted that day, and at supper Jim groaned and took as much trouble in sitting down as if his leg was in splints.

"What's wrong with you?" inquired Hiram, with extraordinary sympathy.

"It's my leg."

"Wal?"

"You know I told you. It's thet place where Hal has been kickin' me every night in his sleep."

"Wha—at?" stammered Hal. His eyes opened wide.

"Lad, I'm sorry to hev to hurt your feelin's," replied Jim, gently. "But I've shore stood it as long as I could. You're one of them nightmare sleepers, an' when you git after anythin', or anythin' gits after you, then you kick. I never seen a broncho thet could hold a candle to you. No matter how you lay, on your side or back or belly, you can kick, an' allus in the same place. I was throwed from a horse onct an' hurt this leg, an' right there's where you've been kickin' me."

Hal looked as if he wanted to cry. He seemed unmistakably, genuinely ashamed of himself.

"Oh, Jim, I know I have crazy dreams and thrash about in my sleep. Why — why didn't you kick back — kick me out of bed?"

"Shore, lad, you needn't feel bad about it. I ain't blamin' you. I realize we're havin' some pretty warm times after these cougars, enough to make any feller hev nightmares."

"I won't trouble you again that way," said Hal, earnestly. "I'll sleep somewhere else. . . . Hiram, can I come in your tent — way over on one side, far from you?"

"Youngster, I wish you hedn't asked me," replied Hiram, in apparent distress. "Fer I've got to refuse. I'm gittin' old, Hal, an' I must hev my rest. You'd keep me awake."

Pride and mortification held Hal back from further appeal. He finished his supper without another word. Then he took the axe and cutting down some small pines began to make a shack. Navvy got so interested that he offered to help, and to our great delight, when the shack was completed Hal pointed to it and asked the Indian to share it with him.

The next day we had some strenuous chases; the hounds split on fresh trails, and we were separated from one another. One by one we got back to camp, and it was a mooted question which were the most worn out, hunters or hounds. It was about dark when Jim came riding in.

"Fellers, you shore missed the wind-up," he said, throwing the skin of a cougar on the ground.

"Wal, dog-gone it, you hed to kill one!" exclaimed Hiram.

"Shore. Curley and Tan treed thet one, an' I yelled fer you till I lost my voice. He started down, finally, an' as I was afraid he'd kill a dog I hed to kill him. When I got the skin I started to work up to the place I left my hoss. It's bad climbin'. I got on a side of a cliff an' saw where I could work out, if I could climb a smooth place. So I tried. There was little cracks an' ridges for my hands an' feet. All to once, just above I heard a low growl. Lookin' up I saw a big lion, bigger'n any we've chased, an' he was pokin' his head out of a hole, an' shore tellin' me to come no farther. I couldn't let go with either hand to reach my gun, because I'd have fallen; so I yelled at him with all my might. He spit at me an' then walked out of the hole, over the bench, as proud as a lord, an' jumped down where I couldn't see him no more. I climbed out all right, but he'd gone. An' I tell you for a minute he shore made me sweat."

That night Hiram whispered to Ken and Jim and me to stay up till Hal and Navvy had gone to bed. We did not need to wait long, and soon Navvy's snores and Hal's deep breathing assured us we might safely talk of our plan.

126

"Youngster, you slip up an' steal Hal's gun," whispered Hiram. "I wouldn't be easy in mind monkeyin' with thet kid if he hed a gun handy."

Ken got down on his hands and knees and crawled noiselessly toward the shack. He did not return for some time. At last he appeared carrying Hal's weapons, and we all breathed easier.

"Thet kid shore has us all buffaloed," remarked Jim.

Then we got our heads together. It was not strange for Ken to be eager to pay Hal back in his own coin, and perhaps I was still young enough to feel the fun of a good, well-deserved trick. But it did seem strange for Hiram Bent and Jim Williams to outdo us in eagerness. Hiram was excited and Jim was bursting with suppressed glee.

"See hyar, youngster, I've planned it all," said Hiram. "Now you take this lasso — thar's a noose on each end — an' jest wrap it once round thet little saplin' thar, an' then slip a noose over Hal's foot an' one over Navvy's."

"You've planned, and I must execute," protested Ken. "By George! Hiram, can't Dick help me?"

"I'll take one end of the lasso," I replied. "That will make it easier for us to wrap the middle of the lasso round the sapling. We'll both walk round it once. Come on."

The sapling in question was about fifteen feet from Hal's shack, and quite in the open. Ken and I got the lasso round it, and then dropping on all fours we crawled stealthily toward the shack.

"You take the Indian," I suggested, in a whisper.

"Good!" whispered Ken. "I'd rather try to rope Geronimo than my kid brother."

Like snails we crept on, as tense and silent as if there were real danger. We reached the shack and lay low a moment. Hal had wrapped himself in his blanket, but the Navajo lay partially uncovered. It turned out that I had gotten the worse of the choice, for Ken soon slipped his noose over Navvy's uncovered foot. And I had carefully to remove the blanket from Hal before I could get the lasso over his foot. Hal kicked, but he did not awaken. I returned to the other conspirators to find Ken already there.

"What next?" I demanded.

"Wal, it's my turn now," whispered Hiram, "an' if you fellers don't see some fun then I'm an old fool."

"What are you going to do?" asked Ken.

"Youngster, I never seen the sleepin' Injun thet I couldn't scare out of his skin, an' you jest listen an' watch."

Hiram got down flat on the ground and began to squirm like a snake, with a perfectly noiseless motion. He went out of sight toward the shack.

We waited, holding fast to each other, straining eyes, and listening with all our might. The silence was unusual, there being only a faint moan of wind in the pines.

Suddenly a hideous ear-splitting sound rose on the night air. It was neither yell, nor roar, nor bawl. Like a prolonged superhuman shriek it pierced us, transfixed us to the spot. It bore some faint resemblance to a terrible loud, coarse whistle.

The shack flew up and tumbled to pieces, out of which bounded the Navajo. His screech of terror rose above Hiram's unearthly cry. Navvy leaped, and then, like a nine-pin, down he went. Hal jumped up, and, yelling, ran the other way, and down he went. Both sprang up and leaped away again, only to go tumbling down. Quick as thought Navvy rose and started to run; Hal, doing the same, ran into the Indian's arms. Then Hiram stopped his unearthly noise. The frightened dogs burst into an uproar. Everything happened so quickly that I could scarcely keep track of it. Down went Navvy and Hal all in a heap.

Suddenly Hiram roared out. "Hyar, you tarnal redskin! stop thet!"

We rushed up to find Navvy sitting astride Hal and pommeling him at a great rate. It was only the work of a moment to rescue poor Hal, after which he roared as loudly as Hiram, but our roaring was laughter.

We had not thought that Navvy would suspect Hal, and that had made our little trick thrice successful.

"How — much — does — it take — to scare you — Hal?" choked Ken.

Hiram added his say: "Hal — I was jest —

wonderin' — what your pa — would hev thought — if he hed seen you."

We did not see any more of Hal till next day. As that was to be a day of rest, particularly for the hounds, we lounged in the shade. Hiram, however, who was seldom idle, spent his time in making buckskin moccasins for the hounds. More or less we all bantered Hal with our several opinions of what it took to scare him. Like a waiting volcano with a cold exterior, Hal endured our sallies in silence. Indeed he did not appear to hold resentment — Hal was not that sort of a boy — but all the same his brain was busy. And we all shivered in our boots. Whatever Hal's feelings were toward us he did not reveal, but he watched the Indian steadily and thoughtfully. By that we knew Hal had designs on Navvy, and we awaited developments with some relief and much interest.

Toward sunset we were interrupted by yells from the Navajo, off in the woods. The brushing of branches and pounding of hoofs preceded his appearance. In some remarkable manner he had got a bridle on Marc, and from the way the big stallion hurled his huge bulk over logs and through thickets, it appeared evident he meant to usurp Jim's ambition and kill the Navajo. Hearing Hiram yell, the Indian turned Marc toward camp. The horse slowed down when he neared the glade and tried to buck. But Navvy kept his head up. With that Marc seemed to give way to ungovernable rage and plunged right through camp; he knocked over the dog-shelter, and thundered down the ridge.

Now, the Navajo, with a bridle in his hands, was thoroughly at home; he was getting his revenge on Marc, and he would have kept his seat on a wild mustang. But Marc swerved suddenly under a low branch of pine, sweeping the Indian off.

When Navvy did not rise we began to fear he had been seriously hurt, perhaps killed, and we ran to where he lay.

Face downward, hands outstretched, with no movement of body or muscle, he certainly appeared dead.

"Badly hurt," said Hiram, "probably back broken. I've seen it afore from jest sich accidents."

"Oh no!" I cried. And I felt so deeply I could not speak. Jim, who always wanted Navvy to be a dead Indian, looked profoundly sorry.

"He's a dead Injun, all right," replied Hiram.

We rose from our stooping postures and stood around, uncertain and deeply grieved, till a mournful groan from Navvy afforded us much relief.

"Thet's your dead Indian!" exclaimed Jim.

Hiram stooped and felt the Indian's back, and got in reward another mournful groan.

"It's his back," said Hiram, and true to his ruling passion, forever to minister to the needs of horses and men and things, he began to rub the Indian and called for the liniment.

Hal went to fetch it, while I, who still believed

Navvy to be dangerously hurt, knelt by him, and pulled up his shirt, exposing the hollow of his brown back.

"Here you are," said Hal, returning on the run with a bottle.

"Pour some on," replied Hiram. Hal removed the cork and soused the liniment all over the Indian's back.

"Don't waste it," remonstrated Hiram, starting to rub Navvy.

Then occurred a most extraordinary thing. A convulsion seemed to quiver through the Indian's body; he rose at a single leap, and uttering a wild, piercing yell, broke into a run. I never saw an Indian or anybody else run so fleetly. Yell after yell pealed back at us.

Absolutely dumfounded, we all gazed at each other.

"Thet's your dead Indian!" ejaculated Jim.

"Dog-gone me!" exclaimed Hiram.

"Look here," I cried, picking up the bottle. "See! Don't you smell it?"

Jim fell face downward and began to shake.

"What?" shouted Hiram. "Turpentine! You idiots! Turpentine! Hal brought the wrong bottle!"

CHAPTER XIII

THE CAÑON AND ITS DISCOVERERS

Hal, however, was not always making trouble. Like Ken, he had a thoughtful turn of mind, and when in this mood he was not slow to seek information.

"What made this Cañon?" he asked.

And I undertook to tell him.

"Well, Hal, I don't see how any one could look at this Cañon without wondering how it was made," I said. "It seems to me the forces of nature were no more wonderful here than elsewhere. But here you can see so much of what's been done, and that makes you curious.

"Ages ago, you know, the whole face of the earth was covered by water. And as the crust began to cool, and shrink, and crumple up, the first land began to rise above the water. In this part of the country the Rockies were the first points of land to appear. As the earth's crust kept on crumpling these mountains kept rising above the water. As they rose they began to weather, and dust, sand, silt, and rock washed back into the ocean, and formed layers on the

133

bottom. This went on for thousands and thousands of years.

"All this time the earth was lifting itself out of the sea, and finally a continent was formed. But it wasn't much like the continent of to-day. Florida and the Southern States were still under water. There was a great inland sea north of this plateau region, and as the uplift continued this inland sea began to flow out, cutting a river into the plateau. This river was the Colorado.

"Probably it rained much harder and longer in those early days, and the river, with its tributaries, had greater power, and there was a greater erosion. The Colorado cut its way through to the Gulf of California. As time went on, and the uplift of land continued, the river cut deeper and deeper, and erosion by rain and wind and frost widened the channel into a cañon. The different layers of rock raised up were of different degrees of hardness and softness.

"Some readily wore away; others were durable. These layers were the deposit of silt into the ocean bed, where they had been burned or cemented into rock strata. There have been fifteen thousand feet — three miles — of strata washed off from the earth here, where we sit now.

"Then the uplift increased, or there was a second and quicker uplift of the plateau. It was greater here, where we are, than southward. That's why the north rim is so much higher. The whole plateau has a tilt to the north. This second uplift gave the river a greater impetus toward the sea, and that, of course, gave it greater cutting power. The narrow inner cañon was thus formed. This drained the inland sea. The river is small now to what it was then. But the same washing, grinding of sand on rock is going on down there And up above the same eroding and weathering of rims."

"Gee whiz!" exclaimed Hal. "It's easy to understand the way you put it. Then these different-colored cliffs, the yellow, and red, and white — they're made out of the sand and silt once washed into the sea, and petrified into the layers — the strata, you called it — and then uplifted, to be washed away again. It takes my breath!"

"Yes, and from these layers we can determine when life first appeared in the sea. For we find shells and bones of a low order of life imbedded in this rock."

"Who discovered the Cañon, anyhow?" asked Hal. "If the fellow rode out of the cedars right upon the rim, without being prepared, I'll bet he thought he'd come to the jumping-off place."

"Ken can tell you that better than I," I replied.

"It's worth knowing, Hal," said Ken. "Look here, who were the first white people in America, anyway?"

"The Jamestown, Virginia, colony in 1607," Hal answered, triumphantly, "and the Plymouth colony in 1620."

Ken laughed.

"Well," said Hal, rather sulkily, "of course, there are all the stories of Norsemen dropping in any old time all the way from Newfoundland to Long Island Sound, but they certain didn't amount to much as settlers."

"No, we won't count the Norsemen," said Ken. "But, Hal, just think of this. The Grand Cañon, away out here in this wilderness, was discovered in 1540, sixty-seven years before the Jamestown colony landed, and eighty years before the *Mayflower* dropped anchor at Plymouth."

Hal whistled.

"That makes Plymouth Rock look young," he said. "Who found the Cañon?"

"It was discovered by a Spaniard. His name was Don Lopez de Cardenas. He was a lieutenant of the great Spanish explorer Coronado, who sent him out from his camp near the so-called Seven Cities of Cibola, usually identified as the Pueblos of Zuñi. Cardenas with a handful of men traveled into northern Arizona, and finally reached the gorge now known as the Grand Cañon. He must have traversed the southerly edge of the Colorado plateau and passed through the Coconina forests."

"I don't understand," said Hal. "These were Spanish warriors in helmets and breasts plates like the men with Cortez in Mexico and Pizarro in South America. What brought them to such an out-of-the-way place as this?"

"It's a romance," replied Ken, earnestly; "but it's a true one, and it goes back to the search for a way to the treasures of the Far East, which led to Columbus' discovery of Cat or San Salvador Island in the West Indies, and then to the Spanish occupancy of Cuba, and to the gold-hunts of De Soto in our South and Pizarro in South America."

"I don't see the connection," grumbled Hal.

"You will in a minute. You see when the Spaniards were settled in Cuba in the early sixteenth century they kept on looking for two things — gold and a water route to Cathay or China and the Spice Islands of the East. Now, in 1528 a Spanish expedition under Narvaez came to grief in Florida. A few survivors made their way across the Gulf of Mexico, and finally four who were left were captured by the Indians a little west of the mouth of the Mississippi. For years they were captives among the Indians of eastern Texas and western Louisiana. They made many long journeys, and their leader, Alvar Nuñez Cabeza de Vaca, gained some favors by acting as medicine man. But at last they escaped. They traveled across Texas and northern Mexico, and in 1536 succeeded in reaching the northern outpost of Spain in Mexico, at Culiacan, in Sinaloa."

"That must have been the first time a white man crossed this continent," broke in Hal.

"Yes, Alvar Nuñez Cabeza de Vaca was the first to cross the continent. He was the first white man to see the buffalo, and another thing he did was to bring back stories of wonderful towns filled with riches of which the Indians had told him. Stories like this had reached the Spaniards before. Within three years a priest, Fray Marcos de Niza, taking one of Alvar Nuñez Cabeza de Vaca's followers, started north to find the Seven Cities of Cibola. He probably did find the Pueblos of Zuñi, but he brought back exaggerated stories. Such stories, especially one of Quivira, an Indian treasure city, led Mendoza, the Viceroy of Mexico, to organize a search expedition which was commanded by Coronado, the Governor of New Galicia. He started north in 1540 with over three hundred soldiers and over a thousand Indian allies and Indian and negro servants. He captured Zuñi, although he didn't find any gold. He wintered there and sent out exploring parties, and one of them, to come back to my starting-point, found the Grand Cañon."

"Did the Spaniards get down into the Grand Cañon?" asked Hal.

"They tried to. Some of the men with Cardenas climbed down a long way with Indian guides. They said that some rocks on the sides of the cliffs which seemed the size of a man from above proved to be larger than the great tower at Seville when they reached them. But they could not go on to the bottom. They estimated the width of the Cañon at the top at three or four leagues."

"But," said Hal, "didn't the Spaniards ever reach the river itself?"

"I should say they did," replied Ken. "Listen. In 1539 some ships commanded by Don Francisco de Ulloa evidently reached the mouth of

138

the river. When Coronado started the next year, the Viceroy sent out another fleet commanded by Don Fernando de Alarcon. This fleet was to go north along the Mexican coast, and as they knew nothing of the geography of the region they thought Coronado and Alarcon would not be far apart and could keep in touch. Alarcon not only reached the mouth of the Colorado, but he ascended the river in boats for eighty-five leagues and called it the Rio de Buena Guia. Also Melchior Diaz, who led an exploring party sent out by Coronado, went across Arizona to the Gulf of California, crossing the Colorado River."

"Where did you get all this?" asked Dick, abruptly, and then, as Ken held up a small book, "Oh! you've been reading up. But my histories never told me this. What is that?"

"That," said Ken, "is Castañeda's 'Relations,' or Journal, and Castañeda was an educated private soldier with Coronado who was the historian of the journey, in order that there might be a full report for the Viceroy of Mexico and the Emperor-King of Spain. It has been translated and explained by Mr. G. P. Winship, and other scholars, like Bandelier, have helped to make the Spanish explorations known. Cabeza de Vaca wrote a full account of his wanderings, like many other adventurous Spaniards."

"Oh! What became of Coronado finally?" asked Hal.

"His expedition journeyed from Zuñi eastward, entered Kansas, and probably reached the northeasterly part of the State."

"How about the golden Quivira?" asked Hal.

"The only Quivira they found was a wretched little village, probably of the Wichita Indians, in Kansas. But here is a dramatic thing. While Coronado was up there in Kansas with his fine expedition, poor De Soto, who had fought his way from Florida to the Mississippi, had crossed the river, and was distant only a journey of a few days for an Indian runner — in fact, it is related that Coronado heard of some white men there in the heart of this strange country and sent a messenger to find them, who failed. Now here's the thing that strikes me. At that early day, in the summer of 1541, two Spanish expeditions, one starting from Florida, and one from Mexico, practically traversed the breadth of our continent, and nearly met in eastern Kansas. We always hear of the Jamestown colony and the Pilgrims; but think of the Spaniards crossing the continent twice in the first half of the century before Jamestown."

"It's a great story," said Hal. "I hope Coronado got some reward."

"Not much," Ken snapped out. "First, he fell from his horse and was badly hurt. Secondly, he had found no gold. That was the important thing. So he reached the City of Mexico in the spring of 1542, 'very sad and very weary, completely worn out and shamefaced.' "

"Didn't he get any credit for his discoveries?"

"Not a particle. Yet he had made known to

140

Europeans a vast territory extending from the mouth of the Colorado River to the Grand Cañon, and stretching east nearly to the Mississippi and north to Nebraska."

"What became of him?"

"He was so coldly received by the Viceroy," answered Ken, "that he resigned as Governor of New Galicia and retired to his estate in Spain, where he died."

"It's a wonderful story," said Hal.

"There's nothing better in the exploration of this country," Ken agreed. "But, Hal, I've talked myself out and it's time to do something else."

CHAPTER XIV

HIRAM BENT'S STORY

How old Hiram Bent was no one knew, and he probably did not know himself. But his life of Western adventure had included Indian-fighting and buffalo-hunting in the early days, and once in a while he could be persuaded to talk of wild life on the plains. Something that he said made us demand a story, and at last he began:

"Youngsters, this narrer escape I had happened way down in the northwest corner of Texas. Jim must know jest about whar it was.

"I was tryin' to overhaul a shifty herd of buffalo, an' had rid mebbe forty or fifty mile thet day. As I was climbin' a slope I saw columns of dust risin' beyond the ridge, an' they told me the direction the herd was takin'. When I got on top I made out far ahead a lone sentinel of the herd standin' out sharp an' black against the sky line.

"When the wary old buffalo disappeared I hed cause to grumble. For there wasn't much chance of me overhaulin' the herd. Still I kept spurrin' my hoss. He plunged down the ridge with a weakenin' stride, an' I knew he was most done. But he was game an' kept on. Presently I saw the flyin' buffalo, a black movin' mass half hid by clouds of whitish dust. They were a mile or more ahead an' I thought if I could git out of the rough ground I might head them. Jest below me were piles of yellow rock an' clumps of dwarf trees, an' green thet I reckoned was cottonwoods. My hoss ran down into a low hollow, an' afore I knowed what was up all about me was movin' objects, red an' brown an' black. I pulled up my snortin' hoss right in the midst of a band of Comanches.

"One glance showed me half-naked redskins slippin' from tree to tree, springin' up all around with half-leveled rifles. I felt the blood rush to my heart an' leave my body all cold an' heavy. There wasn't much chance them days of escapin' from Comanches. But my mind worked fast. I hed one chance, mebbe half a chance, but it was so hopeless thet even as I thought of it I hed a gloomy feelin' clamp down on me. I leaped off my hoss, threw the bridle over my arm, an' with bearin' as natural as if my comin' was intended I went toward the Injuns.

"The half-leveled rifles dropped, an' the strung bows slowly straightened, an' deep grunts told of the surprise of the Comanches.

" 'Me talk big chief,' I said, wavin' my hand as if I was not one to talk to braves.

"One redskin pointed with a long arm. Then the line opened an' let me through with my hoss.

It was a large camp of huntin' Comanches. Buffalo meat and robes were dryin' in the sun. Swarms of buzzin' flies showed the fresh kill. Covered fires gave vent to thin wisps of smoke; worn rifles gleamed in the sun, an' bows smooth an' oily from use littered the grass. But there were no wigwams or squaws.

"I went forward watched by many cunnin' eyes, an' made straight for a cottonwood-tree, whar a long trailin' head-dress of black-barred eagle feathers hung from a branch. The chief was there restin'. I was expectin' an' dreadin' to see a short square Injun, an old chief I knew an' who had reason to know me. But instead I saw a splendid young redskin, tall an' muscular, an' of sullen look.

" 'How,' I said.

" 'How,' he replied.

"Then we locked eyes. I was cold an' quiet, hidin' my fear an' hope. An' the Injun showed in his piercin' glance suspicion thet would hev been astonishment in any one save a redskin. Thet Injun hed a pair of eyes that showed the very soul of lifelong hatred.

" 'Ugh!' he exclaimed. 'White man — buffalo-killer — lose trail. Me know white man!'

"I would have liked to deny my reputation. But thet would hev been the worst thing for me.

" 'No lose trail — come swap pony,' I said.

" 'Heap lie!' he replied, in scorn.

" 'Big chief brave — now,' I taunted, an' swept my arm round the camp. I knew the Injun nature. The chief lifted his head with a motion that said 'No.' The Comanche cared for nothin' but courage an' endurance. He was faced in his home by a defenseless hunter. No doubt he felt the call of his blood. It was his law that he couldn't tomahawk me or order me shot an' scalped till he hed made me show fear. An' thar was my hope. The Comanche hed to see fear in me, or sense it, before he could kill me.

"I looked as if I didn't know what fear was. I jest made myself stone. In this was all the little hope I hed of life. The redskin hed to be made believe I had rid into his camp, feelin' no fear of death, recognizin' no cause for it, an' holdin' myself safe. Now the redskin believed in the supernatural, in the unseen force of nature leaguin' itself with the brave, an' givin' man a god-like spirit. Years of bloody warfare had driven the redskin back from the frontiers, made him a savage whar once no doubt he was noble, but fire an' strife an' blood couldn't stamp out thet belief.

" 'Swap pony,' I said again, an' showed silver I would include in the trade.

" 'How much?' he asked.

" 'Heap much,' I answered.

"He held out a brown lean hand for the silver, an' threw it straight back in my face. The hard silver cut an' bruised me; blood flowed from cuts, but I didn't move a muscle, an' kept a cool gaze level with the dark hot eyes of the redskin.

"Thet flingin' of the silver was a young chief's

undignified passion toward a prisoner who hed become prisoner without effort or risk for any warrior. No honor was thar in me, no glory in insult to me. I caught my advantage, an' became cooler an' stonier than ever, an' put a little contempt in my looks.

"A sudden yell from him brought his band runnin' an' leapin'. They grunted an' let out deep savage cries. A circle formed round us, a circle of bronzed, scarred warriors, an' I felt my time was near. They all knew me, not so much because I hed fought them, but because I was a great buffalo-killer, an' they hated me for thet. More than any other hunter I made meat scarce at their camp-fires. Their meanin' eyes roved from chief to me, spellin' sentences of iron an' torture an' death.

"The Comanche took from one of his braves a long black bow as tall as himself, an' a long feathered an' barbed arrow. He leaned toward me, an' his look was so keen thet I felt it would read my soul.

" 'White hunter lie — no want swap pony — hunt buffalo — no smell Indian smoke.'

"I kept silence an' never let my gaze flicker from his. Thet was all I could do. No word, no move could help me now. I summoned all I had left of courage, an' tried in a flash to think of all the tight places I hed been in before.

" ' White hunter lie!' repeated the Comanche.

"Then with slow an' deliberate motion, never lowerin' his burnin' gaze, he fitted the arrow to the bow an' slowly stretchin' his arms he shot the arrow at my foot.

"I felt it graze me and heard the light thud as it entered the ground. I twitched inwardly an' a chill crept up from my foot. But I made no outward motion, not a flick of an eyelash.

" 'White hunter lie!'

"Thet was the redskin's stumblin'-block. He couldn't believe that any white hunter, much less me, would dare to come before him an' all his braves, an' ask to swap ponies. His crafty mind told him it couldn't be true. An' every beat of his heart throbbed to make me show it. Selectin' another arrow he set the feathered notch against the rawhide cord — an' twang! . . . The sharp point bit into the leather of my boot, an' buried itself half length.

"Thet Comanche's gaze became the hardest thing I ever stood. He looked clear through me for signs of weakenin'. I saw the cold gleam of somethin' hangin' in the balance, an' I matched white courage against red cunnin'. His eyelids shut down till they was mere slits over black blazes, an' the veins over his temples swelled an' beat. Still, he had command of himself, an' his movements were as slow as the torture he promised. Again he reached for an arrow, notched it, drew it, paused while he called me liar, then shot it. A knife-blade couldn't hev been wedged between thet arrow an' my foot. Then, one after another, slow an' cruel, he shot twelve arrows, an' penned my foot in a little circle of feathered shafts.

"With thet he stopped to eye me for a little. Suddenly, as quick as he hed been slow, he shot an arrow straight through my boot, pinnin' my foot to the ground.

"It burned like a red-hot bar of iron.

" 'Heap lie!' he yelled, in a voice of thunder.

"Again he leaned forward to search my face for a shade of fear. But the pain upheld me, an' he couldn't scare me. Then he sprang erect to straighten the long bow in line with his eye. He lifted the bow so that the murderous arrow-head of flint pointed at my heart. An' his eye pierced me. Slow — slow as a fiend he began to bend the bow. It was thick an' heavy, an' hed been seasoned an' strung when firearms were unknown to the redskins. It was such a bow as only a great chief could own, an' one thet only a powerful arm could bend. An' this chief bent it slowly, more an' more every second, till, makin' a perfect curve, it quivered an' vibrated with the strain. The circle of Injuns parted from behind me. Once loosened thet arrow would never have stopped in my body.

"I knew either the Injun or I must soon give way under thet ordeal. But it was my life at stake, an' he began to weaken first. He began to tremble.

" 'Swap pony — lie!' he said.

"Somehow I hed it in me then to laugh.

"The Comanche kept his look of pride an' hatred. Then, raisin' the bow, he shot the arrow in a wonderful flight out of sight over the ridge.

" 'Waugh! Waugh!' he cried in disgust, an' threw down the bow. He couldn't frighten me, therefore he wouldn't kill me.

" 'Brave lie!' A kind of light seemed to clear his angry face. He waved his long arm toward the ridge an' the east, an' then, turnin' his back on me, went among the cottonwoods. The other warriors went after him, leavin' my way open. Thet was how even the Comanches honored courage.

"I pulled the arrows from the ground, an' last the one thet held my foot like a red-hot spike. Leadin' my hoss I limped out of camp, an' climbed the ridge. When I got out of sight I took off my boot to see how bad I was hurt. Thet thar arrow went between my toes, jest grazin' them an' hardly drawin' blood! I hed been so scared I thought my foot was shot half off. . . . But all the same, thet was the narrerest escape Hiram Bent ever had!"

CHAPTER XV

WILD MUSTANGS

One morning Navvy came in with the horses and reported that Wings had broken his hobbles and gone off with a band of wild mustangs. We were considerably put out about it, especially as Hal took the loss much to heart. Hiram asked the Navajo whether the marauding band were really mustangs or the wild horses we had seen on the plateau. And Navvy grinned at the idea of his making a mistake over tracks.

"Shore thought there wasn't no mustangs up here," commented Jim.

"Thar wasn't when we come up," replied Hiram. "They jest trotted down off Buckskin, climbed up hyar an' coaxed Wings off. Wild mustangs do thet a lot, an' so do wild hosses fer thet matter. The mountain's full of them. We're all the time havin' trouble with our hosses. Now a hoss thet's well broke an' tame an' even used to haulin' a wagon will git crazy the minnit he smells them wild hosses. An' he'll git like a fox, an' he'll hide in the cedars when you track him, an' dog-gone me if I don't believe he'll try to hide his tracks."

"Isn't there any way to catch Wings?" inquired Ken.

"I reckon we'll never git a bridle on him agin. But we might round up the band, an' catch a couple of mustangs. What do you say to takin' the trail of them mustangs?"

Ken and Hal yelled their desire for that, and it seemed to suit Jim pretty well. And I was like him, rather pleased to undertake whatever pleased the brothers.

"What'll I ride?" asked Hal, suddenly.

"You an' Navvy can both saddle a pack-hoss," replied Hiram.

"You shore ain't goin' to take the Injun?" inquired Jim.

"Wal, I reckon so. He's a Navajo, ain't he? An' while I don't like to hurt your Texas feelin's, Jim, thar never was the white feller on earth thet could hold a candle to a Navajo when it comes to hosses."

"Shore, you're right," declared Jim, with wonderful good nature.

"An' fellers," went on Hiram, "stuff some biscuits in your pockets, an' throw a blanket on your hoss before saddlin'. Mebbe we won't git back to-night. Ken, give the hounds a good feed, an' see they're tied proper. It'll be a rest for them, an' they need it."

"Shall I take my rifle?" asked Ken.

"Wal, you'd better. Thar's no tellin' what we'll strike down thar in the brakes. It's my idee them

151

mustangs will take to thet wide plateau down below, lookin' fer rich browse. An' thet's jest what I'd like to see. Down thar we'd hev a chance to corner them, an' if they go up in Buckskin thar won't be no use trackin' them."

The hounds howled dismally as we rode away from camp, and the last time I turned I saw Prince standing up the length of his chain and wild to go with us. In a hollow perhaps a half-mile from camp Navvy picked up the mustang trail, and he followed it through the forest without getting off his horse.

"Boys, can you see tracks?" I asked Ken and Hal.

Ken laughed his inability, and Hal said: "Nix."

"Wal, I can't see any myself," added Hiram.

It was remarkable how the Navajo trailed that band of mustangs over the soft pine-needle mats. Try as I might I could not see the slightest sign of a track. However, when we got to the dusty trail at the head of the Saddle, tracks were exceedingly plain to us. We rode down in single file and were glad to find the mustangs had turned to the left toward the plateau that Hiram had called the brakes. We passed the spring and Hiram's camp, where I had brought the boys to meet him, and then went on past the gulch where we had come down.

Before us spread a plateau a thousand feet under the great rim-wall above. It widened and widened till the walls of rock were ten miles apart, and the end of this wild brake was fully thirty miles away. It was an exceedingly wild and rough place. The horses had to go slowly. Scrub-oak only breast-high, and as thick as a hedge, and as spiked as a barbed-wire fence, made progress tedious and painful.

"Ken, you'd hardly think you were down in the Cañon, would you?" I asked.

"It's hard to know what to think down in this awful hole. Where are we, anyhow?"

"There's no name for this bench that I ever heard. It's only a line on the maps. We've just got beyond the end of Powell's Plateau. Buckskin, of course, rises on our right. To the left the real Cañon deepens, and straight ahead — that yellow rim with the black border — is what they call Siwatts. It's spur of the mountain."

The outlook from where we rode was level only at a distance. As we went on we were continually riding up and down ridges, heading cañons and gullies, and crossing brooks. We jumped deer and foxes and coyotes out of every brake. The scrub-oak gave way to manzanita — a red-barked, green-leaved species of brush that was almost impenetrable. And when we did get through that it was to enter a cedar forest where the ground was red and bare and soft. The mustang tracks were now plain to the eye and quite fresh. Other tracks were of great variety. Hiram halted us all round an enormous cougar track. The marks had evidently been made some time before, and during wet weather. The cougar was so heavy he had sunk in half a foot, and his

153

track was bigger around than that of any horse we had.

"I reckon he's the captain," remarked Hiram.

Ken dismounted once to pick up some arrowheads. One was a perfect point, over six inches long, of dark blue flint, and sharp as a blade.

"Thet's pretty old, youngster," said Hiram. "The Navajos used to come here for their buckskin. Thet's why the mountain was called Buckskin."

Hal fired at a coyote, and the sleepy pack-horse he rode woke and nearly left the boy hanging on the spikes of a cedar.

"Hyar!" called Hiram. "Don't shoot fer nothin', Hal. We don't want to scare the mustangs."

The trail led across the cedar forest, out into open ground again, and began to go down, bench by bench, step by step.

It was hot down there. But presently the sun was hidden behind storm-clouds and the air grew cooler. I heard Jim grumbling that he never trailed any horses that did not stop to graze. And Hiram replied that this particular band evidently was making for some especial place. Presently we came out upon the edge of a step with another step some hundreds of feet below. The scene was so rugged and beautiful and wonderful that I had to look many times before I made any special note of ground near at hand. But finally I saw a triangular promontory, perhaps a mile or more in length on each side, and this was green with rich grass and willow except out on the extreme point, where it was bare and white. Deep cañons bounded this promontory on three sides.

"Git back out of sight," said Hiram. "If the mustangs are down thar we don't want them to see us."

We all dismounted and led our horses back into a clump of cedars.

"We'll wait hyar an' let Navajo go look thet place over," added Hiram.

The Indian understood without being told, and he stole off among the jumbles of rocks. Hal was the other one who did not rest, and he got on the trail of some animal and went off among the cedars toward a seamed and cracked cliff. We heard him throwing stones, and presently he yelled for Ken.

"Youngster, hurry up an' sit on thet thar kid, or he'll spoil our mustang hunt," said Hiram.

Navvy returned and announced that he had seen the mustangs browsing. Then Hiram went off with him to get sight of the band and the lay of the ground. Meanwhile the sky grew darker and darker, and there was a cool touch of rain or snow in the air. Hiram was gone nearly an hour, and in that time Jim and I saw or heard nothing of the boys.

"It's goin' to snow," said Hiram. "An' we've got to throw a camp quick. Say, them mustangs are down thar on thet kite-shaped shelf, an' dog-gone me if thar ain't only one trail leadin' down. An' it's narrer an' steep. We can drive them an' ketch all we can handle. Whar are the youngsters?"

"Shore we don't know. They're chasin' somethin' shore's you're born," said Jim.

"Who fetched an axe?" asked Hiram.

I was never caught out without my small hand-axe, and with this we set about cutting cedar branches and brush to make shelters. A big black cloud swooped down on us, bringing a flurry of snow. At that juncture Ken and Hal stalked into camp, each carrying a struggling, snapping little fox. Both boys were bleeding from bites or cuts which they minded not at all.

"Been ropin' foxes, eh?" asked Hiram. "Wal, let 'em go an' pitch in hyar an' help. We've got the mustangs rounded up, an' with good weather we'll hev more fun an' hard work than you youngsters hev seen yet."

It was noticeable that Ken released his capture, while Hal tied his to a cedar with a cord. Both lads lent their aid, and it was not long before we had a big lean-to on the windward side. It was not finished any too soon, for the snow began to fall. A snowstorm like this one was as bad as rain, and as good as rain, too, for it was heavy, thick, and wet. When the storm passed six inches of snow lay upon everything. The sun still hid behind clouds, but the air was warm and the snow melted fast.

"Fellars, it's gittin' late, anyhow," said Hiram.

"An' we couldn't do much in this snow. We'll wait till to-morrer. I'll fence up thet narrer trail so the mustangs can't give us the slip."

We lounged around our camp, made a meal on biscuits and snowballs, and rolled in our blankets to sleep soundly. Hiram awakened us early. We ate what little we had left, and, as the sun rose red and warm, we were eager to begin the day's adventure.

"Let's all take a look at the mustangs," suggested Hiram.

There were patches of snow left in shady places, and the ground was soft and soggy. We followed Hiram out of the cedars, thorough brush and round huge boulders, and finally crawled to a point on the edge of the bluff.

"Look at thet! Jest look!" whispered Hiram, hoarsely.

The bare promontory glistened in the morning sunlight, and right in the middle of it was the band of wild mustangs. There were whites and blacks and bays.

"There's Wings!" burst out Hal.

"S-s-sh. Not so loud thar," said Hiram.

"What are they doing?" asked Ken, in eager interest.

"The snow's melted, an' they're drinkin' out of the little pockets in the rock."

"Well! — it's great!" replied Ken.

I shared his delight. To my mind there could not have been a more beautiful sight than the mustangs drinking on that promontory. The

157

mustangs looked wild. They were shaggy. Long manes waved in the breeze. The leader of the band, a fine, keen-looking white, stood on guard. His attitude showed pride as well as suspicion. He held his head up and he was looking our way. Beyond the promontory yawned the blue shadow of an abyss, and beyond that lifted a bold red bluff, and farther on loomed a great dome. And all around to left and right were the ragged ridges of rock and the dark clefts between the cliffs. It was a wild background for these wild rangers of the wilderness.

"Thet white feller's winded us, I do believe," said Hiram. "Wal, I reckon it doesn't make no difference to us. He can't git out."

"Hiram, may I take a picture of that bunch?" asked Ken.

"Shore. But you must go down through the crack in the rocks thar, an' then crawl as close as you can."

Ken slipped away, and soon returned to us, enthusiastic over his picture and more than enthusiastic over the beauty of some of the mustangs.

"Why, Hal, my mustang is nowhere for looks. And Wings — he's like a dub compared to some of the ponies in that band."

"Wal, it ain't goin' to be an all-fired job to ketch a couple of mustangs," said Hiram. "But what'll we do with them?"

"Shore, let's wait till we ketch some," replied Jim, wisely.

"Hiram, we can turn them over to the Indian," I suggested.

"Thet's so. He'll drag them up on the plateau, an' break them for us."

"How are we going to catch them?" I asked.

"Dick, we've got a place made to order. You all can hide behind an' above thet crack whar the trail comes up. I'll go down an' drive the mustangs up, an' you fellers can rope 'em as they come out."

"Shore it'll be lively round here," chuckled Jim.

"Youngsters, you'd better both lay for Wings an' rope him," said Hiram. "Jim an' Dick can each rope a mustang. Thet'll be enough, won't it?"

"I want to rope one for myself," replied Hal. "I don't care whether we get Wings or not."

"I'd like to pick one out, too," added Ken.

"Wal, I'm sure I don't keer if you rope half a dozen. Every man for hisself, then. Only, youngsters, I'd advise you to put on your gloves, an' tighten your belts, an' git ready for a warm time. It'll be easy to drop a noose over a mustang's head, but holdin' him mebbe'll be another story. Git your lassoes ready, now."

Jim and the brothers took up a position on the side of the gully where we expected the mustangs to come up, and Navvy and I took ours on the opposite side. Hiram rattled down over the stones of the trail, with a last word to the boys to make ready for some real sport.

As I had asked for the loan of Wings from my friend in Kanab, it fell to me as a duty to catch the mustang if I could. We waited for quite a while, and excitement began to verge on strain when we heard Hiram's stentorian yell. Following that was a sound like low thunder, then a sharp clattering, and then the clear ringing of hard hoofs on stone.

"Shore they're comin'," called Jim.

I had expected to see the mustangs run out of that crack in single file. But they burst out, it seemed, three or four abreast, in a cloud of dust and a thundering din. I saw Jim's noose whip over a mustang's head. Then the dusty air appeared full of flying lassoes. The mustangs ran their heads right into the loops. I watched for Wings, but did not see him. In a twinkling the band had cleared the crack and were half across the cedar bench. I heard a confusion of yells and pounding hoofs and crashings in the brush. But I could not see for dust, and had to run to one side out of the thick cloud.

Jim had a white mustang down, and Navvy had a bay well under control. Then I saw Ken. In an instant he was actually dodging the plunges of a vicious pinto. Ken had roped one of the band, but now he did not know what to do, except hold on. That he was doing valiantly at the risk of his life. The pinto reared and, like a furious deer, struck with his fore hoofs. Ken dodged and ran to the extent of his rope and hauled away with all his strength. His quarry began to leap and pull and drag Ken through the brush.

"Hold hard thar, youngster," yelled Hiram. He came running out of the crack in the rocks and quickly laid his powerful grasp on Ken's rope.

"Where's Hal?" I yelled. No one heard me. All were too busy. I turned this way and that. Finally, way off on the bench, at least a hundred yards, I saw a mustang jumping and shaking his head. Then I saw a tight lasso round his neck. I did not wait to see Hal, but started to run with all my might. The mustang, a beautiful slate color with white tail and mane, kept plunging through the brush, and I knew he was dragging Hal. Then I saw the boy. He was down, but trying to get up, and holding to the lasso as if he would die before he let go.

"Hang on, Hal," I cried. "He's a beauty. You've got a prize. Hang on!"

Hal regained his feet. The mustang renewed his fight for freedom. And then began a race. He dragged Hal so fast for a little while I scarcely gained at all. But Hal tripped and fell, and as he would not give up, of course, his weight held the mustang back. I gained ground, reached Hal, and grasped the tight lasso. One jerk sent that savage mustang to his knees and took away some of his breath and fire. He thrashed about and wrestled a few more moments, and then squared away, fore hoofs braced, and, refusing to budge, watched me with wild eyes. Promptly I tied the lasso to a stout bush. Again he began to rear and jump, and as the rope did not give an inch he choked himself pretty thoroughly, and at length fell flat. I hurried up and loosened the noose and tied a knot that would not slip.

"He's ours — Hal; where are you?" I yelled.

It was a sorry-looking lad I found half sitting up in the brush. Dust-covered, scratched and bloody, with his clothes in tatters, Hal Ward was a sight.

"I'm all right except my wrists. They're all skinned from the rope," he said. "Gee! What a pony! Say, Dick, is he hurt? He breathes so hard."

"He's just winded and scared. We'll leave him here till we find out what to do with him. Let's go back."

We returned to camp, where Hal was greeted with solicitude, and then, when it became known that he had not been hurt, there was uproarious mirth at his appearance.

"I don't care. I got the blue-ribbon winner of that bunch," retorted Hal.

So indeed it turned out. Hal's mustang was a beauty, one and all agreeing that he was about the wildest and raciest and most beautiful little horse we had ever seen.

"Wal, I 'ain't noticed thet any of you ketched Wings," said Hiram.

For that matter not one of us had even seen the mustang. Hiram said that it was rather strange, and he went back down to the promontory. Upon his return he told us that Wings was down there and could be readily caught.

"He turned back, I reckon," went on Hiram. "An' now, fellers, let's figure things. We've had a right smart bit of luck. But we can't take all these wild mustangs up on the plateau with us. Let's put them down on thet bench, an' close up this crack so they'll be corralled. Then we can git them on our way back to Kanab."

That appeared to be a wise solution to our problem for the present. Wild mustangs are apt to be white elephants on hunters' hands. So, while Hiram and Jim went down to catch Wings, the Navajo half led and half dragged our captured mustangs down through the crack to the promontory.

"I reckoned," said Hiram, upon his return with Wings, "thet it'd be best to leave the lassoes trailin' on the mustangs. We don't run much risk of one chokin'. An' we can ketch them easy when we come back. Now to build thet corral gate. Everybody rustle for big branches of cedar."

An hour of hard work saw the task completed, and it gave us much satisfaction. Then we mounted and took our own backtrail toward the Saddle and the plateau camp.

CHAPTER XVI

SPLIT TRAILS

When we trooped out of the pines next morning, the sun, rising gloriously bright, had already taken off the keen edge of the frosty air. The ridges glistened in their white dress, and the bunches of sage and the cedars, tipped with snow, were like trees laden with blossoms.

We rode swiftly to the mouth of Left Cañon, into which Jim had trailed three lions. On the way the snow, as we had expected, began to thin out, and it failed altogether under the cedars, though there was enough on the branches to give us a drenching.

Jim reined in on the verge of a narrow gorge, and told us that a lion's cave was below. Hiram looked the ground over and said Jim had better take the hounds down while the rest of us waited above, ready for whatever might happen.

Jim went down on foot, calling the hounds and holding them close. We listened eagerly for his call or the outbreak of the pack, but there was no sound. In less than half an hour he came climbing out, with the information that the lions had left the cave, probably the evening after he had chased them there.

"Well, then," said Hiram, "let's split the pack an' hunt round the rims of these cañons. We can signal to each other if necessary."

So we arranged for Jim and Hal to take Ranger and the pup across Left Cañon, Hiram to try Middle Cañon with Tan and Mux, and Ken and I were to perform a like office in Right Cañon with Prince and Queen. Hiram rode back with us, leaving us where we crossed Middle Cañon.

Ken and I skirted a mile of our cañon and worked out almost to the west end of the Bay, without finding so much as a single track. Then we started back. The sun was now hot; the snow all gone; the ground dry as if it had never been damp; and we complained that our morning was a failure.

We reached the ragged mouth of Right Cañon where it opened into the deep, wide Bay, and rode close to the rim because we hoped to hear our companions across the cañon. The hounds began to bark on a cliff, but as we could find no tracks in the dust we called them off. Queen obeyed reluctantly, but Prince wanted to get down over the wall.

"They scent a lion," I declared. "Let's put them over the wall."

Once permitted to go the hounds needed no assistance. They ran up and down the rim till they found a crack which would admit them. Hardly had they vanished when we heard them yelping. We rushed to the rim and looked over. The first step was short, a crumbled section of wall, and from it led down a long slope, dotted here and there with cedars. Both hounds were baying furiously.

I looked the cañon over carefully and decided that it was a bad place to venture into.

"Ken, it's hard to tell which way the hounds run in these cañons. I think Queen is heading up. Anyway, I'll go that way, and you go down here. We'll get separated, but don't forget the signal yell."

With that I proceeded along the rim to the left, making sure I heard a hound in that direction. It was rough, hard going, and in the excitement of it I forgot how much ground I was covering. I came to a place, presently, where I determined to go down, and leaving spurs, chaps, gun, coat and hat on the rim, I started down, carrying only my lasso. The slope was steep, a long incline of scaly, rotting rock, growing rougher toward the bottom. I heard the baying of a hound, to my right and turned in that direction. Soon I was among huge rocks and windfalls of cedar. Through this it was impossible to keep a straight line. I turned and twisted. But as I continued to hear the baying of the hound I thought I could not be going wrong. In this way time passed, yet still I did not seem to get any closer to the dog, and though I yelled for Ken I got no response. Working more to the left of the dense jumble of weathered rock and thicket of dead cedars I made better progress. All the time, though I appeared to be in the bottom of a cañon, I was descending rapidly. Then the louder baying of the hound and yells from Ken spurred me forward. Another shout guided me to the right, and running through a clump of cedars I came out upon the edge of a deep, narrow cleft.

Up on the opposite slope I saw Queen with her paws on a cedar and above her clung a lion, so close that she could nearly reach him. Prince was nowhere in sight, nor was Ken.

"Ho! Ken!" I yelled.

"Hi! Hi! Dick!" his reply came down the cañon, and both yells blended in a roar that banged back and forth in echo from the cliffs.

I ran up the cañon a little way, to find my passage blocked, unless I chose to go far around. Then I hurried back, only to see that I could not get across below. In my excitement I thought of leaping across and searched for the narrowest place. But the split was quite twenty feet wide and I dared not risk it.

"Ken, I'm on the wrong side of the cañon," I yelled.

"Go back — head it," he replied. "Here's the lion — treed."

"It's too far back that way — it would take an hour to climb round — no help for it."

Then I climbed up a little so as to be on a level with the lion. The cedar that held him was perhaps fifty paces away. Ken came down, and there we were, a few feet apart, in easy talking distance, yet widely separated in so far as any help to each other was concerned.

"Where's Prince? Look out for him. I hear him below. This lion won't stay treed long," shouted Ken.

I, too, heard Prince. A cedar-tree obstructed my view, and I moved aside. A few hundred feet farther down the hound bayed under a tall piñon. High in the branches I saw a great mass of yellow. How I yelled! Then a second glance showed two lions close together.

"Two more! two more! Look! look!" I screamed to Ken.

"Hi! Hi! Hi!" he joined his yell to mine, and for a moment we made the cañon bellow. When we stopped for breath the echoes bayed at us from the opposite walls.

"Waa-hoo!" Hiram's signal, faint, far away, soaring, but unmistakable, floated down to us. Across the jutting capes separating the mouths of these cañons, high above them on the rimwall of the opposite side of the Bay, stood a giant white horse bearing Hiram's dark figure silhouetted against the white sky. They made a brave picture, one most welcome to us. We yelled in chorus: "Three lions treed! Three lions treed! Come down — hurry!"

A crash of rolling stones made us wheel. Queen's lion had jumped. He ran straight down, drawing Prince from his guard. Queen went tearing after them.

"What on earth will we do now?" cried Ken.

"Keep the other lions treed — if you can," I replied, running along the cañon till I neared the piñon tree. Ken clambered over the rocks on his side. We kept yelling for Hiram. Presently Ken was under the piñon, and I at a point opposite. We were now some thirty rods apart, but I was utterly useless to Ken except in the way of advice and encouragement. So for minutes we caught our breath and waited.

"Gee! two big fellows! And they look as scared as I am," called Ken.

"That's good. Keep them scared. . . . I hear Hiram coming. . . . Hi! Hi! This way, Hiram. . . . Ken, just listen to Hiram rolling the rocks. He's coming like an avalanche."

Bits of weathered rock clattered down the slope, and the old hunter was at their heels.

"Whar are the hounds?" he yelled.

"Gone down after the third lion," I replied. "They've treed him down there."

"Wal, that's good. Now you fellers keep these cougars treed. It'll be easy. Bark at 'em like dogs, an' if one starts down, grab a club and run at him as if you was goin' to kill him. Bang on the tree. Beat the branches, an' yell. You can keep 'em up thar till I git back with the hounds."

With that, Hiram, like a giant with seven-league boots, disappeared down the slope. It had all happened so quickly that I could scarcely realize it. The yelping of the hounds, the clattering of stones grew fainter, telling me that

Prince and Queen, and Hiram too, were going to the bottom of the Bay.

"Ken, have you got your gun?" I called.

"No, I left everything but my rope," he replied.

Then the two snarling lions brought me to a keen sense of the reality. Ken had a job on his hands: two almost full-grown lions to be kept treed without hounds, without a gun, without help from a companion.

"Say! this is funny!" yelled Ken. "Dick, I'm scared sick, but I hate to quit. . . . I'll stick. I'll do what Hiram told me to."

It occurred to me then that Hiram probably had not noticed Ken was without his gun, or that I was separated from him by the narrow, deep chasm.

Ken began to bark like a dog at the lions.

About this moment I heard hounds, but could not tell their direction. I called and called. Presently a faint chorus of bays and a yell from Hiram told that his lion had surely treed.

"*Waa-hoo!*" rolled down from above.

Far up behind me, on the yellow cracked rim, stood Jim Williams.

"Where — can — I — git — down?"

I surveyed the walls. Cliff on cliff, slide on slide, jumble, crag, and ruin baffled my gaze. But finally I picked out a place.

"To the left — to the left," I yelled. He passed on with one of the hounds at his heels. "There! let the dog down on a rope and then yourself."

I watched him swing the hound, which I rec-

170

ognized as Ringer, down a wall and pull the slip noose free.

"This doesn't seem so bad," called Ken, who evidently was recovering his nerve. Then he saw Jim above. "Hi, Jim! Where's H-a-l?"

Jim put both hands around his mouth and formed a trumpet. "Hal's lost — somewhere — he an' the pup — split trails."

"Ken, it's going to be a great day — for all of us," I shouted. "Don't worry and stay with your lions."

Then I watched Ringer slide to the edge of a slope, trot to the right and left of crags and turn down in the direction of the baying hounds. He passed along the verge of precipices that made me tremble for him, but, surefooted as a goat, he went on safely, to disappear far to my right.

I saw Jim with his leg wrapped in his lasso sliding down the first step of the rim. The rope, doubled to reach round a cedar above, was too short to extend to the landing below. Jim dropped, raising a cloud of dust and starting the stones. Pulling his lasso after him, he gathered it in a coil on his arm, and faced forward on the trail of the hound. In the clear light, against that wild red-and-yellow background, with the stones and gravel roaring down, streaming over the walls like waterfalls, he seemed another giant, striding on in seven-league boots. I would have called him to come down to help Ken, but it was impossible for him to get to us. From time to time he sent up a yell of encouragement that wound down the cañon, to be answered by Hiram and the baying hounds, and then the strange, clapping echoes. At last he passed out of sight, and still I heard him going down; down till the sounds were only faint and hollow.

Ken was now practically alone with his two treed lions, and I knew that no hunter was ever so delighted. He had entirely recovered from his first panicky feeling. I sat there in the sun watching him. He stood on the slope, just under the edge of the piñon branches, and he had a long club in his hand. The situation was so singular that I could have laughed, but for the peril. The idea of Ken keeping those big cougars treed with a club was almost too ridiculous to consider, yet all the same it was true. For a long time the cougars were quiet, listening. However, as the baying of the hounds diminished in volume and occurrence, and then ceased altogether, Ken's quarry became restless. It was then that he began to bark like a dog, whereupon the lions grew quiet once more.

"That's the way, Ken. You're the best hound in the pack. You've got a fine bark there. Keep it up," I shouted.

As long as Ken barked or bayed or yelped the cougars remained comparatively quiet. Ken, however, began to weaken in voice and finally lost it.

"Dick, you'll have to bark some," he said, and I could scarcely hear him.

At that I willingly began to imitate Prince and

172

Ringer and Mux-Mux. It was easy at first, but soon it became a task. I bayed for an hour. My voice grew hoarser and hoarser, and finally failed in my throat. In order to get out a few bays I had to rest for a moment. Soon I was compelled to stop. The cougars immediately grew restless and then active.

"Ken, you've got to do something," I called, in strained, weak tones.

The lower lion hissed and spat and growled at Ken, and made many attempts to start down. Ken frustrated these by hitting the cougar with stones. Every time Ken threw he struck his mark. Even this punishment, however, did not long intimidate the beast, and he grew bolder and bolder. At length he made a more determined effort, and stepped from branch to branch.

Ken dashed down the incline with a stone in one hand and a long club in the other. I tried to shout advice, but I doubt if Ken heard. He aimed deliberately at the lion, threw the stone and hit him squarely in the ribs. That brought a roar which raised my hair. Then directly under him Ken wielded his club, pounding on the tree, thrashing at the branches.

"Go back! go back!" yelled Ken. "Don't you dare come down! I'll crack your old head."

The cougar came almost within reach of Ken's club. I wondered at the way the boy held his post. Many as were the daring achievements Ken Ward had executed before my eyes, this one eclipsed them all. I was chilled with fear. I was in distress because I could not raise my hand to help him.

Ken must have been in an unreasoning frenzy. He ran round the piñon, keeping directly under the cougar, and intercepting him at every turn. More than once the beast crouched as if to spring, and was only deterred from that by Ken's savage attacks. Finally he had luck enough to give the cougar a ringing blow on the head. This, for the moment, stopped the descent, for the big cat climbed back to his perch beside his mate.

In the momentary lull of battle I heard the faint yelp of a hound.

"Listen, Ken!" I cried.

I listened, too. It came again, faint but clearer. I looked up at the lions. They, too, heard, for they were very still. I saw their heads raised and tense. I backed a little way up the slope. Then the faint yelp floated up again in the dead, strange silence. I saw the lions quiver, and it seemed as if I heard their hearts thump. The yelp was wafted up again, closer this time. I recognized it; it belonged to Prince. The great hound was on the backtrail of the other lion, coming to Ken's rescue.

"It's Prince! It's Prince! It's Prince!" I cried. "It's all up now!"

What feelings stirred me then! Gladness and relief for Ken dominated me. Pity for those lions I felt also. Big, tawny, cruel fellows as they were, they shivered with fright. Their sides trembled. But pity did not hold me long; Prince's yelp, now growing clear and sharp, brought back the savage instinct of the hunter.

A full-toned bay attracted my attention from the lions to the downward slope. I saw a yellow form moving under the trees and climbing fast. It was Prince.

"Hi! Hi! old boy!" I yelled.

Up he came like a shot and sprang against the piñon, his deep bay ringing defiance to the lions.

It was very comfortable, but I felt it necessary to sit down just then.

CHAPTER XVII

STRENUOUS WORK

"Come down now, you cougars," yelled Ken, defiantly shaking his broken club. "I dare you now. Old Prince is here. You can't catch that hound, and you can't get away from him."

Ken had evidently contracted Hiram's habit of talking to cougars as if they were human.

"Oh, Ken Ward, it was tough on you," I said, "and tough on me, too. But we're all right now."

Moments passed. I was just on the point of deciding to go down to hurry up our comrades, when I heard the other hounds coming. Yelp on yelp, bay on bay, made welcome music to my ears. Then a black-and-yellow, swiftly flying string of hounds bore into sight down the slope, streamed up and circled the piñon.

Hiram, who at last showed his tall, stooping form on the steep of the ascent, seemed as long in coming as the hounds had been swift.

"Did you get the lion? Where's Jim?" I asked, in eagerness.

"Lion tied — all fast," replied the panting

Hiram. "Left Jim — to guard — him."

"What are we to do now?" asked Ken.

"Wait — till I git — my breath. We can't git both lions — out of one tree."

"All right," Ken replied, after a moment's thought. "I'll tie Curley and Mux. You go up the tree. That first lion will jump sure; he's almost ready now. The other hounds will tree him again pretty soon. If he runs up the cañon, well and good."

"Wal, thet's a good idee," said Hiram. "Hyar, Leslie, what're you doin' over thar?"

"I couldn't get across," I replied.

"Hev you been thar all the time, leavin' the youngster hyar alone with these critters?"

"Hiram, it couldn't be helped. I was unable to do a blamed thing. But Ken made a grand job of it. Wait till I can tell you."

"Wal, dog-gone me!" exclaimed the old hunter. He pounded Ken with his big hand, then he began coiling his rope. "Ken, you go ahead and tie up Curley and Mux. You, Leslie, git ready to run up the cañon an' keep track of this cougar thet's goin' to jump."

He began the ascent of the piñon. The branches were not too close, affording him easy climbing. Before he looked for even a move on the part of the lions, the lower one began stepping down. Ken yelled a warning, but Hiram did not have time to take advantage of it. He had half turned, meaning to swing out and drop, when the lion planted both fore paws upon his back. Hiram went sprawling down, with the lion almost on him.

Prince had his teeth in the lion before he touched the ground, and when he did strike the rest of the hounds were on him. A cloud of dust rolled down the slope. The lion broke loose and with great, springy bounds ran up the cañon, Prince and his followers hot-footing it after him.

Mux and Curley broke the dead sapling to which Ken had tied them, and dragging it behind them, endeavored in frenzied action to join the chase. Ken drew them back, loosening the rope, so in case the other lion jumped he could free them quickly.

Hiram calmly gathered himself up, rearranged his lasso, took his long stick and proceeded to mount the piñon again. I waited till I saw him slip the noose over the lion's head, then I ran up the slope. I passed perilously near the precipice and then began to climb. The baying of the hounds directed me. In the box of yellow walls the chorus seemed to come from a hundred dogs.

When I found them, close to a low cliff, baying the lion in a thick dark piñon, Ringer leaped into my arms, and next Prince stood up against me with his paws on my shoulders. These were strange actions, and though I marked it at the moment, I had ceased to wonder at our hounds. I took one look at the lion in the dark shade, and then climbed to the low cliff and sat down. I called Prince to me and held him. In case our quarry leaped upon the cliff I wanted a hound to put quickly on his trail.

Another hour passed. It must have been a dark hour for the lion — he looked as if it were — and one of impatience for the baying hounds, but for me it was an hour of enjoyment. Alone with the hounds and a lion, walled in by wild-colored cliffs, with the dry sweet smell of cedar and piñon, I asked no more, only that I wished Ken had been there.

Curley and Mux, yelping as they came, were forerunners of Hiram. I saw his gray locks waving in the breeze, and shouted to him to take his time. As he reached me the lion jumped and ran up the cañon. This suited me, for I knew he would take to a tree soon, and the farther up he went the less distance we would have to pack him. From the cliff I saw him run up a slope, pass a big cedar, cunningly turn on his trail, and then climb into the tree and hide in its thickest part. Prince passed him, got off the trail, and ran at fault. The others, so used to his leadership, were also baffled. But Queen, crippled and slow, brought up the rear, and she did not go a yard beyond where the lion turned. She opened up her deep call under the cedar, and in a moment the howling pack were around her.

Hiram and I toiled laboriously upward. He had brought my lasso, and he handed it to me with the significant remark that I would soon have need of it.

The cedar was bushy and overhung a yellow,

179

bare slope which made Hiram shake his head. He climbed the tree, lassoed the spitting lion and then leaped down to my side. By united and determined efforts we pulled the lion off the limb and let him down. The hounds began to leap at him. We both roared in rage at them, but to no avail.

"Hold on thar!" shouted Hiram, leaving me with the lasso while he sprang forward.

The weight of the animal dragged me forward and, had I not taken a half-hitch round a snag, would have lifted me off my feet or pulled the lasso from my hands. As it was, the choking lion, now within reach of the furious leaping hounds, swung to and fro before my face. His frantic lunges narrowly missed me.

Hiram grasped Prince by the hind legs and pitched him down the slope. Prince rolled a hundred feet before he caught himself. Then Hiram threw old Mux and Ringer and Curley, but he let Queen alone. Before the hounds could climb the slope Hiram roped the lion again and made fast his lasso to a tree.

"Let go," he yelled to me.

The lion fell. Hiram grasped the lasso I had held and then called to me to stop the hounds. By the time I had checked them he had the lion securely tied. This beast was the bold fellow which had given Ken such a battle. He lay now, his sides heaving, glaring and spitting at us.

"Leslie — I'm all in," panted Hiram. "Climbin' them awful slopes — ketches me in the heart. I can't go down agin. Thar's Jim guardin' the first cougar. Ken is watchin' the second, the one I fastened with chain an' lasso to a swingin' branch. An' hyar's the third. Three cougars! . . . Wal, I never beat thet in my life. An' I want the day to be a great success fer Ken's sake."

"Hiram, when you've rested go after the pack-horses. Bring them all and the packs and Navvy, too. You take the hounds with you and leave them in camp. Ken and I will tie up the second lion. Then we'll call Jim up and pack the two lions up here to this one. You meet us here."

"Mind you, thet second cougar's loose except fer collar an' chain. His claws hevn't been clipped. He'll fight. An' it'll be a job to pack 'em up hyar. But I can't climb no more."

"Find your horse and hustle for camp," I replied.

Hiram wearily climbed the slope, followed by the hounds, and I took the back-trail down into the cañon. I noted, now that I was calm, what a long distance we had covered. I made fast time, however, and soon found Ken standing guard over his captive. This lion had been tied to an overhanging branch which swung violently with every move he made.

"Say! did you get the third one?" asked Ken.

"You bet we did."

"Now what?"

"Well, I'll go down until I can make Jim hear. I'll call him to come up with his lion. You stay here till I get back."

181

It was another long tramp down to the edge of that slope, but I reached it and yelled for Jim. He answered, and then I told him to come up with his cougar. I sat down to wait for him, thinking he would be glad of a little help. An hour and a half passed before I heard the sliding of stones below which told me Jim was coming. He appeared on the lower slope carrying the lion head downward. Manifestly he was having toilsome work. He could climb only a few steps without lowering his burden and resting.

I ran down to meet him. He was red of face, wringing wet with sweat, and almost out of breath and patience.

"Shore — I'm 'most — tuck — ered out," he said

We secured a stout pole, and slipping this between the paws of the lion, below where they were tied, we managed to carry him fairly well. But he was heavy, the slope was steep, the sliding stones treacherous, and the task nearly exhausted us. We climbed by the shortest way and so passed to the right of Ken. At last we toiled up to where I had parted from Hiram. Jim fell in the shade and breathed hard.

"Leslie — I — might — git down there — to Ken — but I'd never git back. I'm used to ridin' — a hoss."

So I had to go again alone, and discovered Ken sitting guard faithfully over his charge.

"Wasn't I gone a long while?" I asked. "Couldn't help it, Ken."

"It didn't seem long to me," replied Ken.

That was the difference in time as seen through the eyes of fiery youth and enthusiasm.

"Now to tie that rascal," I said. "It's coming to us, Ken. Hiram didn't pay compliments to this particular cougar. We'll cut a piece off each lasso and unravel them so as to leave enough strings. I wish Hiram hadn't tied the lasso to that swinging branch."

"I'll go up and untie it," replied Ken. Acting upon this, he climbed the piñon and started out on the branch.

"Hold on!" I warned. "I'm afraid you'd better stop. How on earth did Hiram tie that rope there, anyway?"

"He bent the branch down."

"Well, it's bending now, and that darned cougar might reach you. I don't like his looks."

But despite this Ken slipped out a couple of yards farther, and had almost gotten to the knotted lasso, when the branch swayed and bent alarmingly. The cougar sprang from his niche between the tree-trunk and a rock, and crouched under Ken, snarling and hissing, with every intention of leaping.

"Jump! Jump!" I shouted.

"I can't jump out of his reach," cried Ken.

He raised his legs and began to slide himself back up the branch. The cougar leaped, missing him, but scattering twigs and bark. Then the beast, beside himself with fury, half leaped, half stood up and reached for Ken.

I saw his hooked claws fasten in Ken's leather wristband. The lad yelled shrilly. I dashed forward, grasped the lion by the tail, and with one powerful swing I tore him loose and flung him down the slope to the full extent of the rope. Quick as thought Ken jumped down, and we both sought a safer locality.

"Whew!" whistled Ken, holding out his hand.

"It's a nasty scratch," I said, binding my handkerchief round his wrist. "The leather saved your hand from being torn off. He's an ugly brute."

"We'll tie him — or — or —" Ken declared, without finishing his speech.

"Ken, let's each take a lasso and worry him till we both get hold of a paw."

Hiram did a fiendish thing when he tied that lion to the swinging branch. It was almost worse than having him entirely free. He had a circle about twenty feet in diameter in which he could run and leap at will. He seemed to be in the air all the time. He sprang first at Ken, then at me, mouth agape, eyes wild, claws spread. We caught him with our nooses, but they would not hold. He tore each noose off before we could draw it tight. Once I got a precarious hold on one hind paw and straightened my lasso.

"Hold him tight, but don't lift him," called Ken. He held his noose ready, waiting for a favorable chance.

The lion crouched low, his body tense, his long tail lashing back and forth across my lasso. Ken threw the loop in front of the spread paws, now half sunk into the dust.

"Ease up, ease up," said he. "I'll tease him to jump into the noose." I let my rope sag. Ken poked a stick at the lion. All at once I saw the slack in the lasso which was tied to the chain. Before I could yell to warn my comrade the beast leaped. My rope burned as it slipped through my hands. The lion sailed into the air, his paws wide-spread like wings, and one of them struck Ken on the head and rolled him down the slope. I jerked back on my rope to find it had slipped its hold.

"He slugged me one," remarked Ken, rising and picking up his hat. "Did he break the skin?"

"No, but he tore your hatband off," I replied. "Let's keep at him."

For a few moments or an hour — no one will ever know how long — we ran around him, raising the dust, scattering stones, breaking the branches, as we dodged his onslaughts. He leaped at us to the full length of his tether, sailing right into our faces, a fierce, uncowable, tigerish beast. If it had not been for the collar and swivel he would have choked himself a hundred times. Quick as a cat, supple, powerful, tireless, he kept on the go, whirling, bounding, leaping, rolling, till it seemed we would never catch him.

"If anything breaks, he'll get one of us," cried Ken. "I felt his breath that time."

"Lord! How I wish we had some of those fellows here who say lions are rank cowards!" I exclaimed.

In one of his sweeping side swings the lion struck the rock and hung there on its flat surface with his tail hanging over.

"Attract his attention," I shouted, "but don't get too close; don't make him jump."

While Ken slowly manœuvered in front of the lion I slipped behind the rock, lunged for the long tail and got a good hold of it. Then with a whoop I ran around the rock, carrying the kicking, squalling lion clear of the ground.

"Now's your chance," I yelled. "Rope a hind foot! I can hold him."

In a second Ken had a noose fast on both hind paws, and then passed his rope to me. While I held the lion he again climbed the tree, untied the knot that had caused so much trouble, and shortly we had our obstinate captive stretched out between two trees. After which we took a much-needed breathing spell.

"Not very scientific," I said, by way of apologizing for our crude work, "but we had to get him some way."

"Dick, do you know, I believe Hiram put up a job on us?" said Ken.

"Well, maybe he did. We had the job all right. But we'll make short work of him now."

While Ken held the chain I muzzled the lion with a stick and strands of lasso.

"Now for the hardest part of it," said I — "packing him up."

We toiled painfully upward, resting every few yards, wet with sweat, burning with heat, parching for water. We slipped and fell, got up, to slip and fall again. The dust choked us. Unheedingly we risked our lives on the brinks of precipices. We had no thought save to get the lion up.

We had to climb partly sidewise, with the pole in the hollow of our elbows. The lion dragged head downward, catching in the brush and on the stones. Our rests became more frequent. I had the downward end of the pole, and therefore thrice the weight, and I whistled when I drew breath. Half the time I saw red mist before my eyes. How I hated the sliding stones!

"Wait," I panted once. "You're younger — than I — wait!"

At last we dropped our burden in the shade of a cedar where the other lions lay, and we stretched ourselves for a long, sweet rest.

"Wonder — where Jim is?" I said.

Then I heard the lions wheezing, coughing.

"Ken! Look! The lions are choking. They're choking of thirst. They'll die if we don't get water. . . . That's where Jim is — hunting water."

"Water in this dry place? Where will we find it?" implored Ken.

After all our efforts and wonderful good luck the thought of losing those beautiful cougars for lack of a little water was almost sickening.

"Ken, I can't do another lick. I'm played out. You must find water. Don't hope and wait for Jim. Go yourself. It snowed yesterday."

Then into my mind flashed a picture of the

many little pockets beaten by rains into the shelves and promontories of the cañon rim.

When I told Ken he leaped up and ran like a startled deer. I watched him with curious pride and faith. What an athlete he was! He swung up over boulders, he drew himself up by grasping branches, he walked straight up steep slides. The roar of a starting avalanche came from under his heels. Then he reached the rim and disappeared.

For what seemed a long time he remained out of my sight; then he appeared carrying his cap in both hands. He had found water.

He began the downward journey. Like a tight-rope performer he balanced himself on crumbling stones. He stepped with the skill of a goat; he zigzagged weathered slopes; he leaped fissures and ran along yellow slides. The farther down he got, the faster he came, until it seemed as if he had wings. Places that in an ordinary moment would have seemed impassable he sailed over with the light touch of sure feet. Then he bore down upon me with an Indian yell of triumph.

"Ken, old boy, you're a wonder!" I exclaimed.

He grasped a lion by the ears and held his head up. I saturated my handkerchief and squeezed the water into his mouth. He wheezed, coughed, choked, but to our joy he swallowed. He had to swallow. One after another we served them so, seeing with unmistakable relief the sure signs of recovery. Their eyes cleared and brightened; the dry coughing that distressed us so ceased; the froth came no more. Spitfire, as we had christened the savage brute which had fought us to a standstill, raised his head, the gold in his beautiful eyes glowed like fire, and he growled in token of returning life and defiance.

Ken and I sank back in unutterable relief.

"Waa-hoo!" Hiram's yell came breaking the warm quiet of the slope. Our comrade appeared riding down. The voice of the Indian calling to Marc mingled with the ringing of iron-shod hoofs on the stones.

Then Jim, stooping under the cedars, appeared from the opposite direction.

"Hello! Shore I've been huntin' water, an' couldn't find none. Hevn't you seen the need of it?" Suddenly he grasped the situation, and his red face relaxed and beamed.

Hiram surveyed the small level spot in the shade of the cedars. He gazed from the lions to us, and his dry laugh split the air.

"Dog-gone me if you didn't do it!"

CHAPTER XVIII

HAL'S LESSON

It was a strange procession that soon emerged from Left Cañon. Stranger to us than the lion heads bobbing out of the sacks was the sight of Navvy riding in front of the lions. I kept well in the rear, for if anything happened, which I thought more than likely, I wanted to see it. Before we had reached the outskirts of the pines, I observed that the piece of lasso round Spitfire's nose had worked loose.

I was about to speak when the lion opened a corner of his mouth and fastened his teeth in the Navajo's overalls. He did not catch the flesh, for when Navvy turned he wore only the expression of curiosity. But when he saw Spitfire chewing at him he uttered a shrill scream and fell sidewise off his horse.

Then there were two difficulties; to catch the frightened horse and to persuade the Indian he had not been bitten. We failed in the latter. Navvy gave us and the lions a wide berth, and walked to camp.

Hal was waiting for us, and said he had chased

a lion south along the rim till the hound got away from him.

Spitfire, having already been chained, was the first lion we endeavored to introduce to our family of captives. He raised such a fearful row that we had to take him quite a little distance from the others.

"We hev two dog chains," said Hiram, "but not a collar or a swivel in camp. We can't chain the lions without swivels. They'd choke themselves in two minutes."

Once more for the hundredth time he came to the rescue with his inventive and mechanical skill. He took the largest pair of hobbles we had, and with an axe, a knife, and wire nippers fashioned two collars with swivels that in strength and serviceability were an improvement on those we had bought.

Darkness was enveloping the forest when we finished supper. I fell into my bed and, despite the throbbing and burning of my body, soon relapsed into slumber. And I crawled out next morning late for breakfast, stiff, worn out, crippled. The boys, too, were crippled, but happy. Six lions roaring in concert were enough to bring contentment.

Hiram engaged himself upon a new pair of trousers, which he contrived to produce from two of our empty meal-bags. The lower half of his overalls had gone to decorate the cedar spikes and brush, and these new bag-leg trousers, while somewhat remarkable for design, answered the purpose well enough. His coat was somewhere along the cañon rim, his shoes were full of holes, his shirt in strips, and his trousers in rags. Jim looked like a scarecrow. Ken looked as if he had been fired from a cannon. But, fortunately for him, he had an extra suit.

Hal spent the afternoon with the lions, photographing them, listening to their spitting and growling, and watching them fight their chains, and roll up like balls of fur. From different parts of the forest he tried to creep unsuspected upon them; but always when he peeped out from behind a tree or log, every pair of ears would be erect, every pair of eyes gleaming and suspicious.

Spitfire afforded more amusement than all the others. He had indeed the temper of a king; he had been born for sovereignty, not slavery. He tried in every way to frighten Hal, and, failing, he always ended with a spring to the length of his chain. This means was always effective. Hal simply could not stand still when the lion leaped; and in turn he tried every artifice he could think of to make him back away and take refuge behind his tree. He ran at him with a club as if he were going to kill him. Spitfire waited crouching and could not be budged. Finally Hal bethought himself of a red flannel hood that Hiram had given him, saying he might have use for it on cold nights. It was a weird, flaming head-gear, falling, cloak-like, down over Hal's shoulders. Hal started to crawl on all fours toward Spitfire. This was too much for the cougar. In his astonishment he forgot to spit and growl, and he backed behind the little pine, from which he regarded Hal with growing perplexity.

"Youngster, I hev been watchin' you fer the last hour or so," remarked Hiram. "An' I want to give you a piece of advice. Thar's sech a thing as bein' foolhardy brave. You don't seem to reckon that them critters are cougars, wild cougars, an' not pets."

"But I'm not afraid," replied Hal, boldly.

"Wal, I noticed thet. Mebbe you don't know what danger is. Let me tell you a story I read. Thar was a time onct in the old country when officers of the great French army was reviewin' the troops as they marched out to battle. Presently a big corporal strutted by, bold an' important, swaggerin' himself, an' lookin' fight all over.

" 'Thet's a brave soldier,' said one of the officers to Napoleon. The Emperor shook his head, an' said: 'No!' Arter a while a little drummer boy marched by. He was drummin' away fer dear life, as if by drummin' hard he could keep up his courage. But he was white as a sheet, an' his eyes stuck out, an' he was sweatin', an' every step he took seemed to be with leaden feet.

" 'Thar's a brave soldier,' said Napoleon. 'He *knows* the danger.' "

Hiram's story did not appear to have any great effect on Hal. For a while the lad left the lions alone, but presently he was back tormenting them. He was not at all mean or vicious in his teasing; it was simply that they fascinated him

193

and he could not let them alone. Finally, when Hal slipped, in one of his escapes, just eluding Spitfire by the narrowest margin. Hiram ordered him to keep away from them altogether. Whereupon Hal strode off in anger.

"I never seen sich a youngster," explained Hiram.

"Shore he needs a lesson, an' he's goin' to git it," said Jim. "If the boy only hes the temper cooled in him, an' not broke outright, he'll be fine."

Ken gave one of his short laughs.

"That kid is powder, brimstone, dynamite, and chain-lightning all mixed with a compound, concentrated solution of deviltry. Why, he has positively been good so far on this trip."

Hiram groaned.

"Ken, a few years ago you were almost exactly the same kid that Hal is now," I said, with a smile.

"I was not," declared Ken, hotly.

"Youngster, 'pears to me you did some tall scrappin' fer this same bad kid brother," remarked Hiram.

"That's different. I can fight for Hal and still condemn his trickiness, can't I?"

The afternoon passed, then sunset, and the shades spread darkly under the pines; suppertime went by, darkness came on, the camp-fire blazed — and still Hal Ward did not come back. We were not especially worried on this score, but when bedtime rolled around and no Hal, then both Ken and Hiram showed anxiety.

Morning dawned without his return. We had a late breakfast purposely, as we expected him to be in by the time Navvy drove up the horses. But there was no sign of Hal.

"Something has happened to him, sure," Ken said.

Both Jim and I took a different view, agreeing that the lad had slept out for fun, perhaps to cause us concern, and that he would not come in until he was hungry.

Hiram had no comment to make, but it was plain that he did not like the possibilities. Ken showed no desire for lion-hunting, so we did not go out that day. When night came again and Hal had not returned we were at our wits' end. But knowing his singular propensity for tricks, and believing that he would do almost anything in the way of mischief, we still remained in camp, hoping that he would get as tired of the joke as we were, and return.

Next morning Hiram routed us out early.

"Fellars, I think we've been good an' wrong fer hangin' around here waitin' fer the youngster, tricks or no tricks. It's been growin' on me thet somethin' onusual hes come off. We could hev follered his tracks yesterday a tarnal sight better than to-day. Leslie, you an' Ken rim the plateau-wall. Look fer tracks, an' keep signalin'. Jim an' me'll search the pine, an' the cedar thickets, an' the hollers."

"What are you going to search the thickets

and hollows for?" demanded Ken, with wide eyes of misgiving.

When Hiram had no answer for him Ken grew greatly perturbed.

"Hiram, you don't think — it possible — a cougar could have jumped the boy?"

"Possible? Sartinly it's possible. It's not likely, though. But I've knowed more than one feller to be attacked by a hungry cougar. I've hed one foller me, more than onct. . . . Now, youngster, don't look sick thet way. Thet boy hed to hev somethin' happen to him somethin' serious. It was jest plain as the nose on his face. I hope, an' believe, of course, thet we'll find him safe. But you'd better prepare yourself fer a jar."

The expression of Ken's face made me almost sick, too; and what little hope I had oozed out.

"Leslie, you'd better see if any hosses hev come up or gone down the trail at the Saddle," called Hiram, as Ken and I rode off.

"I tell you, Dick, I'm afraid Hiram takes a bad meaning from Hal's absence," said Ken. "He meant by what he said to you that those rangers, Belden and Sells, might have got hold of Hal."

"I hope they have, because then we'd get only a scare, and Hal wouldn't be hurt much. . . . Well, go slow now, Ken, and keep up hope."

We separated at the rim and took different directions. It was high noon when we met again on the other side of the plateau. Neither of us had found a trace of Hal. We turned for camp, hoping against hope that Hiram and Jim would have a different story.

They were both in camp when we arrived, and they ran out under the pines to meet us. It was plain that they hoped to receive the news from us which we had hoped to hear from them.

It was a gloomy meeting.

"I failed to foller Hal's tracks, an' Jim, he failed, too, an' Jim ain't no slouch on follerin' tracks. It would take an Injun —"

The same thought came to us and we all shouted: "Put Navvy on Hal's trail."

Hiram called the Navajo and began to try to tell him, by signs and speech, that Hal was lost and that we wanted his trail followed.

"Me savvy," said the Indian.

He threw the bridle of Ken's mustang over his arm, and then, bending over the faint imprints of Hal's boots, he slowly walked into the forest leading the mustang.

"Don't foller him. Let him alone," said Hiram, as Ken and I pressed forward.

The Navajo's snail-like progress was intolerable to watch, yet it was hopeful, too, for it meant that he was able to pick out Hal's trail. A long hour passed before Navvy disappeared in the forest. Another passed, still longer. And a third went by that seemed interminable.

"Wal, them desert Navajos hev the sharpest eyes in the world fer a trail. . . . Youngster, he'll find your brother."

Suddenly I saw a black streak darting in the forest.

"Look!"

It shot across an open space, disappeared, came in sight again. It was a horse.

"Wild hoss, I'm afeard," said Hiram.

"No, it's the mustang," said Jim. "I guess mebbe I hevn't often seen a redskin pushin' a mustang to his limit."

"Oh! it's Navvy," exclaimed Ken. "Look at him come!"

"Youngster, now you're seein' some real ridin'," said Hiram.

The beautiful black mustang swept toward camp at the speed of the wind. He ran on a straight line, sailing over logs, splitting through the bunch of juniper with flying mane and tail. The dark Indian crouched low and rode as if he were part of the mustang. There was something wild in that fleet approach, something thrilling and full of hope. The Navajo gained the camp circle, pulled up the mustang until he slid on his haunches, and leaped from the saddle.

We crowded toward him. He said a few words in Navajo, which none of us could translate. There was no telling anything from his dark, impassive face. Then he made motions with his hands and his meaning became at once clear. Hal had fallen over the rim.

"Oh! Oh!" cried Ken Ward, covering his face with his hands.

It was a black moment for all of us. Hiram

and Jim glanced compassionately at Ken, but I could not bear to look at him. As I turned away I saw the Indian pick up two lassoes and a canteen.

"Tohodena! Tohodena!" ("Hurry — hurry!"), said the Navajo.

That put new life into us.

"Look, Ken, the Indian's grabbed up canteen and ropes. That means Hal is alive."

Ken's face seemed transfigured. He darted for Hal's mustang, which was with our other horses, threw on a saddle and buckled it with nervous haste. We were mounted as soon as Ken. Navvy swung his quirt and the race was on. It was a race and a mad one to keep the Indian in sight. Our lion chases were tame beside this wild ride. The pines blurred all about me; the brown sward seemed to shoot backwards under me; the wind howled in my ears. I kept close at the heels of Hiram's thundering roan. The Indian with marvelous skill held to a straight line. Logs and thickets and hollows, even deep gulches did not make him swerve. Once I got a good look ahead, and there was Ken riding Wings almost a rod ahead of Jim, who had a lead over Hiram. I thought at the moment how proud Hal would have been of Wings. But fast as Ken was driving him the pinto could not catch the mustang.

The pines thinned out and clumps of cedar appeared with patches of sage. The Navajo reined in, leaped off, and waited till we raced up. In a twinkling we were off ready to follow.

He carried the lassoes and the canteen.

We were directly above a cape of crumbling rim rock. To me the great abyss, with its purple clefts and gold domes and red walls, had never appeared so sinister and menacing. The Indian led down a short slope of sage and then went out upon a jutting section of wall. This cape appeared to be cut up into crags and castles and columns of yellow stone. One crumbling mass resembled a ruined pipe-organ of grand proportions. We wound in and out, always dangerously near the precipice, following the rim-wall of this cape. The Indian halted upon the edge of a kind of cove, a cut-in some fifty yards across at the widest, where it opened out into the chasm. I saw that the wall on the opposite side was perpendicular and almost forty feet high.

Navvy dropped to his knees and leaned over the rim. We followed suit. I found myself looking down at a straight wall, then a narrow shelf of débris, and below that a small grassy plot of ground which sloped to the main rim-wall.

Ken Ward let out a bursting yell of joy. Then I saw Hal lying on one side of the plot. There was a bloody wound on the side of his cheek and temple.

"Ah, there!" he said, faintly, and he smiled a smile that was as feeble as his voice.

I could not tell what the greeting was we shouted down to him, for the reason that we all shouted at once. Then we leaped up from the rim, ready for action. The first thing Ken Ward did was to give the Navajo such a hug that I made sure he would crush the Indian's ribs. Navvy smiled at this rough treatment as if he knew what it meant to lose and find a brother.

"Cool down now, youngster," said Hiram, "an' let me engineer this bizness."

Jim was more agitated than I had ever seen him. He kept peeping over the rim.

"Hiram, he shore ain't moved a hand or foot since we got here," whispered Jim.

"Mebbe he's too weak," replied Hiram.

The old hunter carefully tied up two lassoes, then two more, and putting these together he made a double rope more than fifty feet long.

"Ken, we'll let you down," he said, running a noose under Ken's arms.

With Hiram and Jim holding the rope Ken slipped over the rim and soon reached the shelf below.

"Hal, old boy, are you hurt — very much?" asked Ken, as he knelt by his brother.

"Water! Water!" whispered Hal.

"Pitch me the canteen, quick," called Ken. Hiram took it from Navvy and carefully poised it.

"Make sure, youngster. It might hit a rock an' bounce down the slope."

"Pitch it!" cried Ken in scornful distraction. "Have I played ball all these years for nothing? Pitch it!"

"Thar," called Hiram, and he pitched the canteen. Ken caught it with steel-like clutch, and then he was kneeling by Hal, holding up the boy's head and helping him to drink. From the length of that drink Hal must have been pretty thirsty.

"Hal, tell me now — where are you hurt?" asked Ken.

The boy whispered something that only Ken heard. And we saw that Ken began to feel for broken bones and search for injuries.

"Hiram, all I can find is the bruise on his face and a bad ankle. It's black and blue and swollen out of shape. I'm afraid it's broken. He can move all over, so his spine can't be hurt."

"Good! Now, youngster, you take off your coat an' put it round Hal, under his arms, whar the rope goes. . . . Thar, thet's right. Now you lift him an' git him straight under us. . . . Steady now. . . . Help me lift him, Jim. An' Leslie, you stand ready to grab him when we git him up."

In less than two minutes we had Hal lying on the rim above. I hardly recognized his face. It was pallid except for the bloody bruise, and his eyes were deep-set with a strained expression of pain, and his lips were drawn. He had changed terribly.

"Oh, I'm all — here," he whispered. But it was only a faint likeness of his old spirit.

"Say! throw me the rope," yelled Ken.

Hiram threw it over, and, while he and I held firmly, Ken came up hand over hand.

"Leslie, you lead back an' break a trail through the brush," directed Hiram, as he carefully lifted

Hal in his arms. We were not long in getting to the horses. Here Hiram placed Hal astride his roan, and walked, with an arm steadying the lad, while Jim rode alongside and helped. This procession was very slow in reaching camp.

When we arrived there, Hiram made a thorough examination of the boy and to our great relief announced that there were no serious injuries.

"He's got a knock on the side of his head, an' a sprained ankle, an' mebbe he's sufferin' from shock, but he'll be around in a few days."

We washed the blood from Hal's face and bathed his ankle in hot water. His face was so painful and his lips so swollen that it was difficult for him to eat, but after he had forced down some potato soup and a few mouthfuls of coffee he appeared to gather a little strength. We were so overjoyed to have him back alive and comparatively well that all thought of his delinquencies had been forgotten. But, evidently, Hal had not forgotten, for he looked wistfully at Ken and Hiram. It appeared to me that Hal wanted to be helped out in his confession. None of us, however, asked him a question.

"Ken," he said, finally, and his voice was strangely weak, "I ran off bull-headed mad, but I didn't stay away for spite. I chased some kind of a young animal — a young coyote, I think — and I fell over the rim."

"Forget it," replied Ken, cheerfully.

"I yelled and yelled," went on Hal. "Then I

knew you wouldn't be hunting for me, because you'd all figure I was playing a trick, trying to scare you. So I stopped yelling. The pain wasn't so bad. I could have stood that. But the thought of you not hunting for me for a long time — that hurt. It made me sick. Then after the first night and the next day I got thirsty. I had a fever, I guess, for I was flighty. Pretty soon I believed — you'd never find me. Then — then —"

He never completed that sentence, but his look was eloquent. Hal Ward had been face to face with his first real tragedy in life. The lesson that Jim had prophesied had been a terrible one.

"Ken," he said, after a long silence, "I broke my promise to you. One thing I did promise, you know. That was to be careful."

"It's all right, kid," replied Ken.

"Jim," he went on, after another silence, "I guess you won't let me 'rustle' with you — any more?"

"Shore I will — shore," replied Jim, hurriedly, as he fumbled aimlessly with his pipe.

Then there was a third silence, this one the longest.

"Hiram," said Hal, "do you remember — you called me a young Injun once, and then I heard you say the only good Injun was a dead one?"

"Wal, lad, what about it?" asked Hiram, kindly.

"When I lay down in that dark hole, at night, with the stars shining in my face I never slept a wink — I thought of what you had said — of your advice — and I made up my mind if I ever got out alive I'd fool you about being a good Injun. . . . I'm goin' to be one."

"Amen," cried Ken Ward, fervently.

CHAPTER XIX

KEN AND PRINCE

Next morning Hiram was out bright and early, yelling to Navvy to hurry with the horses, calling to the hounds and lions and routing us from warm blankets.

Navvy had come into his own: he received his full meed of praise from all of us. Even Jim, reluctantly feeling the place in his hip where he carried a pellet of Indian lead, acknowledged that Navvy had been invaluable. "Shore, he's the only good redskin I ever seen, an' I guess I'll hev to change my mind about liftin' his scalp."

"Tohodena!" said Navvy, mimicking Hiram. Perhaps we all contrasted this jocular use of the word with the grim meaning he had given to it the day before.

As we sat down to breakfast he loped off into the forest, and before we got up the bells of the horses were jingling in the hollow.

"Shore, it's goin' to be cloudy," said Jim.

"If it's just the same to you fellows, I'll keep camp," remarked Hal.

"Wal, lad, I reckon so," was Hiram's reply.

Indeed, we carried Hal out of Hiram's tent and propped him up with blankets. It would probably be several days before he could use his injured ankle. He was haggard, and the bruise had grown blacker. But the terrible, strained shadow of pain in his eyes had given place to something brighter and softer.

"Shore I'm goin' to keep camp with you," drawled Jim, presently.

"That will be fine — but Ken and Hiram and Dick will need you."

"They can need an' be darned. I'm tired climbin' out of them gashes. My heart ain't right yet, after luggin' thet cougar eleven miles or less straight up in the air."

"Wal, youngster," said Hiram to Ken — it was strange and incomprehensible why he called Hal "lad" and Ken "youngster," but so it was — "I reckon we've got more sassy cougars right now than we can pack off this plateau. Packin' them out — thar'll be some fun."

"Everything yet has been fun except some of my stunts," replied Hal.

After breakfast we made a comfortable lounging place for Hal and left him in care of Jim. Then Ken, Hiram, and I rode down the ridge to the left of Middle Cañon. All the way we had trouble with the hounds. First they ran foul of a coyote, which was the one and only beast they could not resist. Spreading out to head them off, we separated. I cut into a hollow and rode to

207

its end, and there I went up. I heard the hounds and presently saw a big white coyote making fast time through the forest glades. It looked as if he would cross close to me, so I dismounted and knelt with my rifle ready. The coyote saw me and shied off. I sent several singing, zipping bullets after him, which only served to make him run the faster. Remounting I turned toward my companions, now hallooing from a ridge below.

The pack lost some time on old trails, but we reached the cedars about eight o'clock, and as the sky was overcast with low dun-colored clouds and the air cool, we were sure it was not too late.

Soon we were in the thick of dense cedars. There, with but a single bark to warn us, Prince got out of sight and hearing. While we separated to look for him the remainder of the pack hit a trail, and then they were off. I kept them in hearing for some time. Meanwhile Hiram and Ken might as well have vanished off the globe for all I could see or hear of them. Occasionally I halted to let out a signal.

"Waa-hoo!"

Away on the dry air pealed the cry, piercing the cedar forest, splitting sharp in the walled cañons and clapping back and forth from wall to wall, rolling on to lose power, to die away in mocking silence.

I rode to and fro, up this gully and down that one. I rimmed what seemed a thousand cañons and yelled till I was out of breath, but I could not find a trace or hear a sound that belonged to my companions or the hounds.

So I turned my horse toward camp, and it was noon when I got there. About three o'clock Curley came in, foot-sore and weary. Next was Queen and she could scarcely touch her crippled foot to the ground. An hour after her arrival Ringer came in. He was worn out, dusty, and panting with thirst and heat.

"Shore everybody was huntin' fer himself to-day," remarked Jim.

At five o'clock Hiram's gaunt charger snapped the dead wood in the hollow. The tall hunter got off and untied two cougar skins from the back of his saddle.

"Whar were you an' the youngster?" he demanded. "Thet's what I want to know."

"I lost you both and couldn't hit your trail again," I replied.

"Wal, the hounds got up cougar chases fer themselves to-day. Prince lit out an' thet settled it. I lost 'em all but Mux an' Tan."

As he spoke the two hounds limped into camp.

"I reckon Ken is sittin' under a cedar, holdin' Prince, an' yellin' fer us to come an' help him git his cougar. . . . It's been another queer huntin' day. Dog-gone it! this plateau is a curious split-up place, an' no wonder we can't do nuthin'. I hed to kill the two cougars I treed, arter I waited hours fer you an' Ken. . . . Wal, I'll rest a little an' then git supper."

"Gee! Hiram, I hope Ken's all right," exclaimed Hal, anxiously.

"Don't you worry, lad. He'll be ridin' in soon."

Hiram had just taken the steaming supper off the fire when the barking of the hounds announced Ken's appearance. He rode wearily under the pines and Prince trotted wearily behind.

"Jest in time, youngster," called the old hunter, cheerily.

Ken fell rather than dismounted, and he slipped to the ground and stretched out so slowly, so painfully, so gratefully, that it was easy to see what he had been through. His clothes were in tatters and he was white and spent. To our solicitations he whispered: "Wait!" And he lay there for full five minutes before he crawled to the supper-cloth.

We were all curious, and Hal was wild to hear Ken's adventure. There was something about Ken Ward, before a time of stress, or after hard action, that thrilled one with its significance. When supper was over and we sat in a circle round the ruddy camp-fire, with the cool wind singing in the pines and the shadows of night darkening, Hiram said: "Wal, youngster, I reckon we want to hyar about it."

Ken was still silent and there was a brooding grimness about his thoughtful face. As we waited for Ken to take his time Prince edged nearer the fire — for the air was chill — and when the great hound laid his splendid head on Ken's knee and looked up with somber eyes, the boy seemed to burst out involuntarily: "Prince saved my life!"

"He did?" breathed Hal, his shining eyes full on his brother. "Tell me — everything!"

Ken settled back and began his story.

"Sometime this morning I lost Hiram and the hounds. I found myself in a dark, gloomy forest. After a while this forest got all but impenetrable. Dead cedars lay in windfalls; live cedars, branches touching the ground, grew close together. I lost my bearings. I turned and turned, crossed my own back-trail, which I followed, coming out of the cedars at a deep cañon.

"Here I fired my revolver, but no answering shot came. There was nothing for me to do but wander along in the hope of finding Hiram or Dick. I was riding on when I saw Prince come trotting to me.

" 'Hello, old boy,' I said. Prince seemed to be as glad to see me as I was to see him. He flopped down and panted with a dripping tongue jerking out of his mouth. He was covered with dust and flecked with froth.

" 'All in, Prince?' I asked. 'We'll rest awhile.' Then I discovered blood on his ear and found the ear slit. He had been pushing a cougar too hard that morning.

"I filled my hat with water from my canteen and gave Prince a drink. Four times he emptied the hat before he was satisfied. Then he laid his head against me and rested.

"Prince got up finally of his own accord, and with a wag of his tail set off westward. I kept my mustang as close to Prince as the rough going permitted. We came out in the notch of the great curve we had named the Bay. I was just about to shout for you when I saw Prince with his hair bristling. He took a dozen jumps, then yelping broke down the steep gorge and disappeared.

"I found a fresh track of the big lion that we have chased so often, and decided to follow Prince. I tied my mustang and took off my coat and spurs and chaps, and fastened a red bandana to the top of a dead cedar to show me where to come up on my way back.

"I went down about five hundred feet until a precipice stopped me. From it I heard Prince baying and almost instantly saw a lion in a tree-top.

"That roused me and I yelled, 'Hi! Hi! Hi!' to encourage Prince.

"I thought it would be wise to look before I leaped. The Bay lay under me, a mile wide where it opened into the big smoky Cañon. It seemed like an awful, bottomless pit. I tell you for a moment the sight shook my nerve, but I had to go after Prince. I ran along to the left and came to where the cliff ended in a weathered slope.

"Once started in dead earnest, it was like playing a game that had to be won. My boots struck fire from the rocks. I slid and hung on and let go to slide again. I started avalanches of weathered rock and then outfooted them.

"But soon I had to go slower and climb over things. Prince bayed once in a while, and I yelled to him to let him know I was coming. A white bank of decayed limestone led down to a runway, where I made up time. Here Prince's bay kept me going. Flying down this to a clump of cedars, I ran in among them and saw Prince standing with fore paws against a big cedar. I saw a lion moving down. Then the crash and rattle of stones told me he had jumped. Prince ran after him.

"I dashed down, dodged under cedars, and threaded openings in the rocks to come to a ravine with a bare, water-worn floor. Patches of sand showed the tracks of Prince and the lion. Those of the lion were so large they made my blood run cold. They were twice the size of any tracks I had seen before. Running down this dry stream-bed was the easiest going yet. Every rod or so the stream-bed dropped from four to ten feet, often more, and these places I slid down.

"The cougar didn't appear to tree any more. I feared every moment to hear the sounds of a fight, for I remembered that Hiram had said an old cougar would get tired running and stop to kill the hound.

"Down, down, down I went. I saw that we were almost to the real jump-off, the great, wide main cañon, and I wondered what would happen when we reached it. Suddenly I came upon Prince baying wildly under a piñon on the brink of a deep cove.

"Looking up I had the fright of my life. The cougar was immense and so old that his color was almost gray. His head was huge, his paws short and round. He did not spit, nor snarl, nor growl; he did not look at Prince, but kept his half-shut eyes on me.

"Before I had time to move he left his perch and hit the ground with a thud. At first I made sure he intended to attack me, and I jerked out my revolver. But he walked slowly past Prince and without a moment's hesitation leaped down into the cove. A rattling crash of sliding stones came up with a cloud of dust. Then I saw him leisurely picking his way among the rough stones.

"Prince came whining to me, and together we went along the cove till we found a place where we could get down. We crawled and jumped and fell till we reached the bottom, and again Prince took the trail.

"Almost before I knew what I was about I stood on the second wall of the cañon, with nothing but thin air under me. I tell you it made me gasp.

"Prince's bark came to me, and I turned round a corner of cliff wall and saw him on a narrow shelf. He was coming, and when he got to me he faced about and barked fiercely. The hair on his neck stuck up.

" 'Come on, Prince,' I called.

"That was the only time I ever knew of Prince hesitating to chase a lion. I had to coax him, for he didn't like that narrow shelf. But, once started, he wouldn't let me lead. The shelf was twenty feet wide, and close to the wall were lion tracks in the dust. A jutting corner of cliff wall hid my view. I peeped round it. On the other side the shelf narrowed and it climbed a little by broken steps. Prince passed the corner, looked back to see if I was coming, and went on. He looked back four times, and once he waited for me to come up with him.

" 'I'm with you, Prince,' I kept calling.

"The shelf narrowed till it was scarcely three feet wide. Prince stopped barking, then looked back for me. A protruding corner shut me from sight of what lay beyond. Prince slipped round. I had to go sidewise and my fingers bit into the wall.

"To my surprise I found myself on the floor of a shallow wind-cave. The lion trail led straight across it and on. Prince went slower and slower.

"I rounded the next point, and crossed another shallow cave, and slipped by another corner to come upon a wonderful scene. The trail ended there. In the center of a wide shelf sat the great lion on his haunches, with his long tail lashing out over the precipice. When he saw us he turned round and walked the whole length of the shelf with his head bent over. He was looking for a place to jump. Then he stopped and bent his head so far over the abyss that I thought he would fall.

"All at once I thought of my camera, and at the same time forgot all about Hiram's telling me never to take my eye off a cougar when at close quarters. I got my camera, opened it, and focused for about twenty-five feet.

"Then a wild yelp from Prince and a roar from the cougar brought me to my senses. The cat leaped ten feet and stood snarling horribly almost in my face. His lashing tail knocked little stones off the shelf. I pulled out my revolver and aimed, once, twice, but was afraid to shoot. If I wounded him he would knock us off the shelf.

"It was then I got scared and began to shake so I could scarcely keep my knees from sinking under me. But good old Prince was braver than I, and he had more sense. He faced the lion and bayed at him.

" 'Hold him, Prince, hold him,' I yelled, and I took a backward step.

"The cougar put forward one big paw. His eyes were now purple blazes. I backed again and he stepped forward. Prince gave ground slowly. Once the lion flashed a yellow paw at him. It was frightful to see the wide-spread claws. In the terror of the moment I let the lion back me clear across the front of the wind-cave, where I saw, the moment it was too late, I should have taken advantage of more space to shoot him.

"The cougar was master of the situation. I kept backing step by step, and I saw the shelf narrowing under my feet. When I remembered the place where it would be impossible for me to back around I almost fainted. I stopped stock still and almost tottered over the precipice.

"Somehow Prince's bravery gave me a kind of desperate strength at the last. The lion, taking slow, cat-like steps, backed Prince against my knees. The great brute was within his own length of me, so close that I smelt him. His eyes fascinated me. Hugging the wall with my body, I brought up the revolver, short-armed, and, straining every nerve, I aimed between those eyes and pulled the trigger.

"The cougar's left eye seemed to vanish with the bellow of the revolver and the smell of powder. He uttered a hoarse howl, and rose straight up, towering over me, beating the wall heavily with his paws.

"I stood there, helpless with terror, forgetting my weapon, fearing only that the beast would fall over on me and brush me off the shelf. But in his death agony he bounded out from the wall, turned over and over, and went down out of sight.

"I had to sit down then. I was all in. The relief made me sick. I sat there with Prince's head on my knees, and slowly got back my strength. Finally, when I tried to rise, my legs were still shaky and I felt as weak as if I were just up from a long sickness. Three times I tried to go round the narrow place. On the fourth I braced up and went around, and soon reached the turn of the wall.

"I was six hours in climbing out. . . . And I guess I've had enough cougar chasing to do me for a while."

CHAPTER XX

AROUND THE CAMP-FIRE

"Wal, youngster," began the old hunter, after a long silence, "I allus reckoned thet Prince was a great hound. An' it's only when a feller gits out alone with a dog an' gits in lonesome or dangerous places thet he really knows how human a dog is."

"Oh! it was grand of Prince to stay between Ken and the lion," exclaimed Hal.

"Shore it's a shame thet hound'll hev to be killed by a cougar some day," remarked Jim.

"I reckon now thet day'll never come," replied Hiram.

"Why? Shore you always said so."

"Prince shall never put his nose to another cougar trail, an' he's goin' back to Pennsylvania with the youngster."

"Hiram! do you really mean to give him to me?" asked Ken, in glad surprise.

"Wal, I reckon so. I'll miss him, but Ringer is comin' on, an' will lead the pack."

"Hiram — it's good of you — I'll —" Ken left off and hugged Prince by way of reply, and

218

the hound licked his face. For once Hal did not look jealous over Ken's possession of something that he could not hope to rival for himself.

"Ken, if you have enough cougar hunting, what next?" I asked.

"The rest of my time here I'll put in studying forestry, and I want you to help me. I declare, I've completely forgotten my work. But I'll make it up. I'm a fine ranger, eh?"

"Wal, youngster, a ranger's duties are many," replied Hiram. "Now, if the Chief was to ask you about cougars, same as he asked you about forest-fires last summer, you could tell him a few things."

"I guess I could," declared Ken.

"Your time hasn't been wasted, an' now thet nobody has been hurt bad or any hosses or hounds killed I feel pretty happy about the hunt. From now on, while I'm hyar on the plateau, I'll tree cougars an' kill 'em, fer I've orders to clear the preserve of them, you know. Meantime you will be addin' to your knowledge of trees, an' Hal will be gittin' well. I calkilate he ought not to ride down these trails fer two weeks. Thet will be long enough for his ankle to git strong. Then we'll pack our cougars out to Kanab. An' we've got to stop down in the brakes at our corral, an' ketch our wild mustangs. We've most forgot them. It'll be some fun — thet job."

"Ken, are you going back to college this fall?" I asked.

"Yes, but I intend to get ahead of my term

219

and take some time off — about January and February — to go South. I want to see the tropics, to study the jungle timber and vegetation."

"Shore you'll look up some trouble down there," said Jim. "I've been in Mexican jungles, along the Rio Grande. Millions of things to shoot."

"Ken, I'm going with you," declared Hal.

"You're going to start in college," said Ken, severely.

"Do you suppose I'd be any good in college with you somewhere in the jungle? Wait till I see father. He'll let me go."

"You'd have a fine chance ever getting to go to any wild place again — if I told him how you jumped over the rim of the Grand Cañon just to scare your brother and friends!"

"I didn't — I didn't," denied Hal, vehemently. "I fell over — and I knocked some sense into me, too. . . . But, Ken, you'll never tell the governor, will you?"

"Lad, I reckon Ken won't give you away," said Hiram. "Fer he an' all of us believe thet adventure has taught you the difference between fun an' foolhardiness. I'd trust you now, an' if I would, surely your brother would. . . . Now, Leslie, you spring your little surprise on the boys."

I turned to Ken and Hal, then hesitated.

"Hiram," I said, "are you sure the Indian can't understand English? I don't want even a word

220

of this to get to any ears but ours."

Ken Ward leaned forward, with his eyes suddenly flashing dark, and Hal sat up in glowing curiosity. Hiram sent the Navajo off to bunch the horses.

"Well, boys, it's this," I began. "Hiram and Jim and I are not going to sign contracts with the Forest Service for next year. We think we've got something a little better. We've found traces of gold down in the Cañon, and we believe there's enough gold to pay us to go after it. And there are chances we may strike it rich. . . . So next summer we want you both to come out and go with us — after gold."

Ken Ward uttered his ringing shout and Hal looked the wild joy that his speechless tongue could not utter. That was their answer.

"Wal, wal, somehow I kinder thought you'd like the idee," said Hiram, as he filled his pipe. "We all want you to come bad. Thar'll be some of the real thing — 'specially if any of them no-good fellers like the one Ken licked git wind of our enterprise. Wal, I reckon we'd hev to fight. How about thet, Jim?"

"Shore, shore," replied the Texan.

So the three of us talked and planned while Ken and Hal drank in every little word.

Meanwhile the camp-fire died down to a small red blaze and the shadows darkened under the pines. Prince went to sleep with his head on his new master's knees. From the captive lions came an occasional soft-padded, stealthy step and a low growl and a clink of chain. The wind began to moan. A twig snapped, and the lithe figure of the Indian strode out of the forest gloom.

"Sleep-ie, Navvy?" asked Ken.

"Moocho," answered the Navajo.

Then he began to prepare his bed for the night. Selecting a spot close to the campfire, he dug out a little pit in the pine-needles and threw a blanket over it. He kicked off his shoes, lay down and curled up with his back and the soles of his bare feet toward the heat. It seemed to me that the moment he had pulled his other scant blanket over his shoulders he went to sleep.

The red light of the dying fire shone on his dusky face and tangled black hair. Ken Ward watched him, and so did Hal. Lying there, covered with his old blanket, there was Indian enough and wildness enough about him to suit any boy. By and by, as we all sat silent, Navvy began to mumble in his sleep.

"Shore I'll hev to scalp thet Injun yet," declared Jim.

"Dog-gone me if he ain't got a nightmare!" ejaculated Hiram.

"No, I think he's dreaming of the adventures we'll have next summer," said Ken Ward.

Ken's idea pleased me. And long after the others had gone to bed, no doubt to dream with the Indian, I sat wide awake beside the ruddy embers, and dreamed, too, of the summer to come. It would be a wild trip — that hunt for gold down in the cañon. With Ken Ward along it would be sure to develop dangers; and with Hal Ward along it would be sure to develop amazing situations.

So I dreamed on till the fire burned out, and the blackness gathered thick, and the wind roared in the pines.

We hope you have enjoyed this Large Print book. Other G.K. Hall & Co. or Chivers Press Large Print books are available at your library or directly from the publishers.

For more information about current and upcoming titles, please call or write, without obligation, to:

G.K. Hall & Co.
P.O. Box 159
Thorndike, Maine 04986 USA
Tel. (800) 257-5157

OR

Chivers Press Limited
Windsor Bridge Road
Bath BA2 3AX
England
Tel. (0225) 335336

All our Large Print titles are designed for easy reading, and all our books are made to last.